ELVEN AND THE PUZZLE BOX

Gwen Lee is a Singapore-born, US-based author of eight children's books. Her award-winning work *Little Cloud Wants Snow!* was a recommended selection at the Read! Singapore Festival and is used by schools in the United States to educate children about weather science. Her other publications such as *There Was a Peranakan Woman Who Lived in a Shoe*; *Elizabeth Meets the Queen: A War Heroine's Journey*; and the *Greco and Beco* series have been featured by institutions such as the National Library Board, Building and Construction Authority, and Singapore Global Network in their outreach campaigns. Gwen is a graduate of University College London and lives in the San Francisco Bay Area with her family and pet chickens.

ELVEN
AND THE
PUZZLE
BOX

Gwen Lee

PENGUIN BOOKS

An imprint of Penguin Random House

PENGUIN BOOKS

Penguin Books is an imprint of the Penguin Random House group of
companies whose addresses can be found at
global.penguinrandomhouse.com

Published by Penguin Random House SEA Pte Ltd
40 Penjuru Lane, #03-12, Block 2
Singapore 609216

First published in Penguin Books by Penguin Random House SEA 2024

Copyright © Gwen Lee 2024

All rights reserved

10 9 8 7 6 5 4 3 2 1

This is a work of fiction. Names, characters, places and incidents
are either the product of the author's imagination or are used fictitiously,
and any resemblance to any actual person, living or dead, events or
locales is entirely coincidental.

Please note that no part of this book may be used or reproduced in any manner
for the purpose of training artificial intelligence technologies or systems.

ISBN 9789815204810

Typeset in Baskerville by MAP Systems, Bengaluru, India

This book is sold subject to the condition that it shall not, by way of trade or
otherwise, be lent, resold, hired out, or otherwise circulated without the publisher's
prior consent in any form of binding or cover other than that in which it is
published and without a similar condition including this condition being imposed
on the subsequent purchaser.

www.penguin.sg

For my best friend Jessica

Contents

1. Scholarship Day — 1
2. Satisfactory Is an Understatement — 11
3. The Wood and Letter — 19
4. An Adventure Beckons — 25
5. The Town of Love and Gold — 31
6. A Reason for Love — 39
7. Takuno's Trick — 49
8. Mama Monga — 57
9. A Sentimental Man — 65
10. A Chance Encounter — 71
11. The Keeper of Birds — 85
12. The Road to the Lake — 93
13. Abe and the Revelation — 103
14. A Riddle Disguised — 109
15. The Unexpected Visitors — 117
16. Revelations in the Dark — 129
17. The Moles — 135
18. Of Bugs and Lies — 143

19. When the Tree Bleeds	149
20. Midnight Horrors	159
21. The Alchemist and the Brave	169
22. The Hand of Fatima	177
23. Hideout and Beyond	181
24. Old Ties and Rivalries	193
25. The Evil Mountain Witch	203
26. The Purveyor of Dreams	209
27. The Mob	215
28. Friends in High Places	221
29. The Truth about Witchcraft	229
30. The Villain Unmasked	239
31. The Temptation of Sticky Yam Balls	245
32. A Flower in Bloom	253
Epilogue	261
Acknowledgements	265

1

Scholarship Day

Elven swung open the heavy cast iron door and peered into the oven. Hot air rose to her face, turning her cheeks a vivid pink. The rainbow cake was perfect. The three-hour wait was well worth it. She smiled to herself. Today, she would be chosen. Today, she would finally escape the orphanage.

Positioning her fingers to avoid the holes in her padded mitts, she removed the tray from the oven and placed it on the counter. Yes, the indigo and violet layers had just the right amount of pigments to differentiate them from each other. And the red no longer reminded her of a fire-engine but of the soft feathers of a rosefinch. After months of fine-tuning the recipe, she had finally mastered the seven layers of the rainbow cake.

'Elven, you slowcoach, where are the pastries?' Jade was standing at the kitchen door, glaring at Elven with her hands on her hips. 'The meeting starts in fifteen minutes. Fifteen minutes,' she yelled. 'Don't you get me into trouble.'

Elven sighed. Ever since Jade had been appointed the housekeeper, her bossiness had gone off the charts.

'Just a minute,' Elven said, laying her masterpiece out on the cooling rack. Jade looked as if she was going to say something sarcastic. Instead, she grabbed the metal serving trolley and pushed it next to the table. Elven loaded up the plates of freshly baked pastries. Other than the almond cookies, which she knew the orphanage director loved, she had prepared some of her most popular recipes—sticky rice with mango, buko pie using fresh, young coconuts from the garden, and pandan cake.

'Don't think I can't see what you're up to,' Jade said with a smirk. 'You think you're going to bake your way into a scholarship, don't you?'

'No more than Mina is trying to garden her way out of here.' Elven had peeked into the staff lounge earlier and was shocked by the number of flowers there. Mina had practically turned the room into an arboretum to showcase her horticultural skills.

Jade gave her a withering look. 'You think it's so simple?'

'It doesn't hurt to try, especially since I'm too old to be adopted.' Elven suppressed a yawn. This morning, she had started work at three, two hours ahead of her usual waking time.

'You got that second part right,' Jade sneered.

'Good,' Elven said as she piped swirls of chocolate onto the plates. She refused to be drawn into an argument with the older girl.

'Actually, I take that back.' A meaningful look crossed Jade's pimply face. 'It's not always about age. You people should know that.'

A large dollop of chocolate squirted across the plate, ruining the delicate curves Elven had just drawn.

You people?

Elven exhaled slowly, deflating the urge to refute the annoying whispers about her background. Ignoring Jade's taunting look, she placed the piping bag on the table and reached for a rag. With swift, deliberate strokes, she began wiping the plate clean.

'Well, I guess the scholarship doesn't matter to you,' Elven said after her pulse rate returned to normal. 'You'll be sixteen soon.'

Jade gave a bitter smile. 'How old are you?'

'Twelve.'

'No wonder you're so uptight.' She sauntered over and pinched a slice of pandan cake off the trolley before Elven could stop her. 'Let me give you a piece of advice,' Jade drawled. 'Stop trying to show off. Your cakes will ruin you.'

Ordinarily, Elven would argue, but there was no time. She hastily arranged the rainbow cake onto the cake stand. Still warm, but it would have to do. She loaded a teapot onto the trolley and made for the doorway.

'Cakes come before a fall, darling,' Jade called out behind her.

Elven bit her tongue and concentrated on steering the uncooperative trolley out of the kitchen. A few doors down in the laundry room, two young girls were talking animatedly as they folded the brown uniforms into wicker baskets. As Elven passed, their chatter stopped abruptly.

As if I'd report you to the caretakers, Elven thought. She felt obliged to say something reassuring to them, but the words were stuck in her throat.

Just then, a child's scream rang down the dim corridor. The girls jumped visibly and threw themselves back into their chore. Elven pushed on, stealing a glance at the toddlers' room as she passed.

A little boy of two was squatting in a pool of pee with a rag, wailing even as he made a clumsy effort to clean it up. Leaning against the unpainted wall, a stone-faced caretaker looked on as she tapped her wooden cane against the table.

Elven turned away, her heart pounding. She was glad she had no memories of her own potty training.

Further up the hall, a girl was standing on a stool outside the candle room, her homely face wet with tears. Inside the dim, windowless room, the seven-year-olds were hard at work, their arms pumping up and down as they dipped their wicks into double boilers full of wax.

'My goodness,' Elven whispered, flinching at the round, red welts on the girl's arms. 'Have you been standing here since breakfast?'

The girl whom everyone called Clumsy Chloe nodded and sniffed loudly.

Against her usual instincts, Elven removed a cookie from the stand and pressed it into Clumsy Chloe's hand.

Chloe's dull eyes popped open and she made as if to say something. But Elven stopped her with an irritated shush and moved on quickly, her trolley clattering across the minefield of potholes along the corridor.

She should never have taken that risk. But what was done was done. And now she could only hope that Chloe was smart enough not to tell anyone.

Walking past the old library, she was reminded of her teacher Mr Singh. Five years ago, when the orphanage still had wealthy benefactors supporting it, Mr Singh had been hired from the capital to 'improve their lives', as the caretakers used to say. For three years, Elven looked forward to his instructions and read-aloud sessions in the library. Mr Singh taught them to ride the bicycle and even brought them on a day trip to the landing site of their great founder, Abel Tanzania. Despite her attempts to be inconspicuous, Mr Singh often sought her out and tried to engage her in his lessons.

'How would you like to be an explorer?' Mr Singh had asked her. 'How would you like to discover an island, just like how Abel discovered Kalimasia?'

When she had blushed and said it was impossible, given her lot in life, Mr Singh told her stories about some of their country's most luminous founding fathers—all of them orphans.

But the good things never last. The money had soon dried up, and Mr Singh was sent away. The library was padlocked, its books sold to the rag-and-bone man. There was no more talk of learning.

Finally, Elven arrived at the entrance of the staff wing. Leaning her weight against the heavy teak door, she tugged the unwieldy trolley onto the thick green carpet. The door swung close.

Silence.

She hurried down the hallway into another world. A world of sunlight, mould-free walls, and plush rugs.

Elven manoeuvred the trolley into the staff lounge, past the sofas to the table in front of the fireplace. Soft piano music was playing from the gramophone and the teal and metallic wallpaper seemed to shimmer and dance in the light streaming through the windows. Jade had chosen a silvery blue, floor-length tablecloth and blue china to match the violet hydrangeas Mina had arranged above the mantelpiece.

The office in the far corner was empty. Even the director's room had its door closed. Thank goodness the committee was late.

Elven set down the plates and teapot, humming to the familiar tune that was playing. She liked how everything was coming together to make this beautiful room extraordinary. As the smell of flowers intermingled with that of warm pastries, she could almost believe that she was in a real house.

'I thought it was you!'

Elven spun around, startled.

'Coal!' she cried. 'What are you doing here?'

'Relax, I didn't shoot a poisoned arrow into Mrs Bayou's back.' He smiled, showing his big white teeth.

Elven laughed, even though his joke about the old caretaker was getting stale. She liked the older boy from the kitchen, not just because they spent so much time cooking together but also because his sunny disposition often made her life more bearable.

'There were a bunch of heavy packages,' Coal continued. 'She told me to bring them to the office for her, that's all. Even offered me a hog jerky in return.'

'Oh God, did you eat it? I wish she'd stop making us try her Mavarian food. Just because I'm darker skinned like the Mavarians doesn't mean I like hog jerky.'

Coal laughed. 'You think too much. Me? I'd eat anything.'

'No wonder she likes you so much.'

'Yes, she does,' Coal answered, suddenly solemn. 'And that's the only reason why she hasn't snitched on me.'

'You mean she knows about your trips to the forest?'

'I think so.' Coal shrugged. 'Otherwise, why would she *casually* mention that the broken fence would be repaired tomorrow?'

Elven gulped. 'You'd better make something Mavarian for dinner tonight.'

'That's my plan. Anyway . . .' Coal thrust something into her hands. 'This parcel's for you.'

Elven stared at the small package wrapped in thick brown paper. She had never received a letter before, let alone a parcel.

'TO THE GIRL WITH ELEVEN FINGERS.' The words were printed in large uppercase letters. It was for her, all right. There was a boy with only five fingers (the other arm ended at the elbow) and another girl with twelve toes. But she was the only one who had eleven fingers. Or at least that was what the extra stump protruding next to her left thumb made it look like.

'Don't you even want to open it?' Coal asked, looking amused by her dumbfounded expression.

Elven touched the stiff corners where the papers had been folded in, not quite sure what to do. 'But why would anyone—'

'Mind if I?' Coal interrupted, his hand hovering dangerously close to the pandan cake.

'Stop!' Elven slapped his hand away.

'All right, all right,' Coal said, looking hurt. 'I know, it's your big day.'

Elven gave him an apologetic smile. 'Maybe you should take the parcel back to the office. I don't want to be caught with this. Not today.'

'As you wish.' Coal shrugged. 'But don't blame me if you never see it again.'

'What do you mean?'

'I've seen Hammond burn letters in his fireplace,' Coal whispered.

'What letters?'

'Letters addressed to the children.'

'But that's ridiculous!' Elven exclaimed in disbelief. 'Why would he do that?'

'Why wouldn't he? Don't you find it strange that none of us ever receives a letter?'

'Of course not. We're orphans. People don't even know we exist.'

Coal raised his left eyebrow in a dramatic arch. 'That's not true. Our orphanage choir is famous across the country. Now, isn't it odd that none of our talented singers ever get any mail from their admirers? Why don't they get adopted? Why is it always the disabled kids who get picked?'

'But it's not about being famous,' Elven sighed. 'The adoption committee looks at our character. Those disabled children are good.'

'Good? With what?'

Suddenly, they heard footsteps coming down the corridor, followed by the unmistakable, high-pitched laugh of the orphanage director. Coal and Elven stared at each other, their mouths open in horror.

'Quick! Over here!' Elven whispered. She lifted the heavy, jacquard fabric covering the rectangular table, and they dived under.

2

Satisfactory Is an Understatement

'But Mrs Monteiro,' said one of the committee members, 'you are too modest! Everyone knows your choir boys are the best in Kalimasia. Why, even the governor's wife has been asking after them since that remarkable rendition of "Ave Maria".'

'Well, I do hope we get invited back this year.' The head caretaker's voice rang loud and clear across the room. 'I rather liked the caviar.'

A low growl escaped Coal's stomach. Elven tried her best to glare at him in the dark, but he shrugged his shoulders to protest his innocence. She turned her attention back to the adults. Judging from the banter, the committee was in good spirits. Elven counted six voices, four of which were unfamiliar.

'Look at that spread,' a woman said. 'You really spoil us, Director Hammond.'

Elven's heart leaped. Someone had finally noticed her efforts. She closed her eyes and muttered a silent prayer.

Please, please, please let me get on the list.

The footsteps closed in on Elven and Coal. Suddenly, the adults were milling around the table, their legs bumping against the tablecloth. Elven shrank back against the fireplace, but poor Coal, who seemed to have developed some kind of cramp, could only watch the fabric swell and ebb inches in front of his legs. With the back of his head resting against the table top, he looked like a contortionist trapped in a magician's box.

Above them, the tinkling of cutlery against china plates punctuated a man's tedious monologue about his award-winning tea plantation in the Southland. Earl Grey tea was offered to and gratefully accepted by the visitors. The women chatted about the latest fashions. Teacups were set on saucers. The squelching of sofa seats. Soft munching. Appreciative murmurs. Then, they began talking business.

'Once again,' said Director Hammond. 'I would like to thank Headmaster Morodon-Gore for taking time off his busy schedule to join us here today. Goldsmith College is one of the finest boarding schools to emerge in our country of late and according to what I've heard from the headmaster, the most progressive in its curriculum. I have no doubt its scholarships will transform the lives of the lucky ones selected today.'

'Thank you for your kind words,' the headmaster replied. 'The pleasure is all mine.'

'Today, we will award scholarships to three children from the nine-to-twelve age group. If you turn to page two of your report,' Director Hammond continued, 'you'll find the names of the children we've pre-selected. Do take a look and let me know if you have any objections.'

Pre-selected? Elven's stomach tightened.

There was a brief rustling of papers.

'Are these the only ones who meet Goldsmith's criteria?' the headmaster asked.

'Well, no but—' Director Hammond's voice was pinched. '—I'm afraid the others are Mawoli, sir.'

'Pity,' the headmaster replied.

Poor Mawolis, Elven thought, *they get left out of everything.*

It was a well-known fact that the Mawolis were considered the lowest race of society. But how they got there in the first place had always been something of a mystery. All Elven knew was that Kalimasia had been overrun by barbaric and feuding Mawoli tribes before Abel Tanzania arrived in 1643. If not for the Western settlers and missionaries who brought law and order, their country would have remained a paradise lost. Or at least that was what the caretakers had drummed into her.

'One can't be too careful about these things,' Mrs Monteiro added.

Elven's heart skipped a beat. Had the nasty gossip about her being half Mawoli reached the director's ears?

'Well, at least we take them in,' the tea plantation man chimed in. 'Not many institutions can make that claim.' The group murmured their assent.

'On pages three and four, you'll see the boys and girls Mrs Monteiro has shortlisted,' said Director Hammond. 'High on our list for the sports scholarships are Ryan and Joseph.'

Ryan and Joseph! Elven thought. *Of all people!*

Elven shot a look at Coal, who made a face back. No, she must have heard wrong. There was nothing outstanding about them. On the contrary, Ryan was a bit of a bully who loved teasing her about her extra finger and Joseph, on his best days, was insipid.

'Why those two, if I may ask?' the headmaster said.

'They are our strongest boys,' replied the director in a constipated voice. 'We think they have the potential to be very good rugby players.'

'I see,' the headmaster said after a short pause. 'This Joseph is a bit on the tall side, don't you think?'

'Oh, is being tall undesirable?' trilled one of the women. 'I thought everyone likes tall boys!'

'No, no, not undesirable,' the headmaster said, his voice terse. 'Just that tall boys can be a little . . . intimidating. We wouldn't want our students to feel threatened by the newcomers, would we?'

'Indeed not!' Director Hammond said, soothingly.

There were coughs and more rustling of papers as the committee members examined their folders.

'Well, how about Matthew, then?' suggested the tea plantation man. 'He's the shortest.'

'A sturdy lad,' Director Hammond chimed in.

'Splendid,' the headmaster replied. 'Matthew it is, then.'

Elven felt the blood rush from her head. How could they give the spot to Matthew just because he was the shortest? This was ridiculous! She felt a gentle jab from Coal. He was looking at her, mouthing the words 'never mind'. Elven glared at him and buried her head in her knees.

'Perhaps Mrs Monteiro would like to give us her top picks?' she heard Director Hammond say.

'Uh-huh,' came the head caretaker's muffled voice. She sounded as if she had too much pastry in her mouth. 'I recommend . . .' Mrs Monteiro coughed and cleared her throat. 'I recommend an older child for the final slot, if only to spare myself the torture of dealing with one too many pre-teens,' she said to bemused chuckles. 'Now, we have three twelve-year-old girls with us—Elven, Mina, and Ginger.'

At the mention of her name, Elven jerked her head up. There was hope yet!

'Let me give you a quick summary,' continued Mrs Monteiro. 'Mina is our head gardener with a bit of a stutter. Nothing serious. The lovely flower arrangement around you is testament to her skills. Ginger works in the janitorial department. She's hardworking and fit as a horse. Finally, we have Elven with her eleven fingers. She's our baker. I hope you find her pastries satisfactory?'

'Satisfactory is an understatement,' exclaimed one of the women. 'They are simply divine!'

'Many fingers make light work!' quipped the tea plantation man to laughter.

Coal rolled his eyes to show camaraderie with Elven. But, for once, she was too nervous to be offended by the joke.

'Undoubtedly,' said another committee member. 'These cakes are the best I've eaten in years!'

Elven covered her mouth lest a squeal of joy escaped from her. She turned to Coal, eyes sparkling. It was the first time anyone had praised her. Recognition at last!

'Well then, we can't afford to lose her, can we?' boomed the tea plantation man. 'What will we eat when we visit at Christmas?'

'Baked beans?' Mrs Monteiro teased.

The room broke out into raucous laughter. Someone even asked if Elven's plum pudding was any good. Before she knew it, the conversation had moved on. Not one person stood up for her.

How dare they eat my food and laugh at me? Elven thought, her fists clenched.

Before she knew it, she was a mess of hot tears and shudders. As she struggled to contain her sobs, she felt Coal's strong arm around her, drawing her close. Elven buried her wet face in his shirt, her hand clutching its stiff fabric like a lifeboat. It was all she could do to keep herself from screaming.

The rest of the discussion went by in a blur. Elven did not know who they chose in the end, although she suspected that it was Ginger. After all, anyone else could mop and dust when Ginger was gone.

Jade was right. Her cakes had ruined her.

When at last the room was empty, Elven crept out from under the table, dazed. All her life, she had believed that her hard work would pay off one day. Now, Elven realized that she had never really stood a chance in this arbitrary system.

'You all right, Elv?' Coal crawled out beside her with a groan. 'I have to get started on the meal preparation before Cook complains.'

He pressed the small parcel into her hands. 'I'm not taking this back. It's yours.'

She blinked. 'But what do I do with it?'

'Whatever you do, don't let them take this away from you.'

Elven watched as he climbed out of the window and made his way across the garden. After a while, she slipped the parcel into her apron pocket. Then, taking an almond cookie into her hand, she tightened her fist around it until it began to crumble.

3

The Wood and Letter

The day passed slowly. By the time Elven finished her chores, it was close to sunset. Keen to avoid the scholarship winners in the dining hall, she decided to skip her evening meal and head out to the secluded spot behind the garden shed.

After making sure that she was alone, Elven took out the parcel from her apron. She stared at the smudged postmark under the fading light, hoping to make out the sender's location. Finally, she stuck her fingers under the folded flap and gave it a determined tug. The paper fell apart to reveal a green felt bundle tied together with string.

Inside the bundle, she found an envelope and a rectangular wooden block about the size of her palm. The top of the block was divided up like a checkerboard of three by five squares. Occupying the fifteen spaces were fourteen wooden tiles. Four of the tiles were blank. The remaining ten each had a letter, which together spelled out the words 'YOU ARE MINE'.

Each word occupied a row. On the first row next to the word YOU was an indentation caused by a missing tile.

Elven ran her thumb across the surface and, quite unexpectedly, the tiles slid across under her touch.

A game! she thought, a thrill running down her spine.

She pushed the tiles around for a while but did not have the slightest clue as to what she was supposed to do. She turned the block around. The sides had intricate veneers inlaid with pieces of timber in different shades of brown. In the bottom right corner, an inverted and blunted v was carved into the wood.

She shook the block and heard something move inside. She wondered if it was a box, but even after careful examination, she found neither hinges nor any means to open it.

Elven laid the block down on her lap and pried open the envelope. Inside, she saw a sheet of thick, good quality writing paper covered in neat cursive handwriting.

My dear girl,

You would not remember me, being barely a day old when we met. I am your grandfather and your mother was my only child. As with all only children, she was headstrong and ultimately disappointing. When she was seventeen, she eloped with a good-for-nothing Native. Soon after I disowned her, the scoundrel squandered her money and disappeared into the night. Your mother was a proud one and she did not come to me for help. If she asked, I would not have been the kind of man to turn away a daughter heavy with child.

But I digress. You must be wondering why I am writing to you after so many years. I am terminally ill, my child. The lump in my brain is growing as I write, threatening to extinguish me in all my loneliness. When one is as close to death as I am, it is time to take care of unfinished business.

Ever since she was a little girl, your mother loved brain-teasers of all sorts. So, it was no surprise that she chose to leave you this handcrafted Puzzle Box. Her last words were: 'She shall find love if she opens it.' You were all she cared about, all she fretted about. As for me, she would barely spare me a smile. It was clear she hated me even in her final hours.

So, you will understand why you had to go to the orphanage. Your deformity is God's accusation against me—a reminder of my sins. I have committed too many treacheries in my lifetime, wronged too many people, and made too few amends.

It is too late to make things up to you, but I am finally ready to let go.

The box is yours, as are your mother's secrets. May you find a way to open it, for God knows I have tried.

Yours,
T.N.

Elven felt a tightness in her chest. She made an effort to breathe, but her exhalation came out as ragged and thin as a piece of torn paper. After so many years, her family had finally contacted her. But who would have thought it would be her mother's father?

Even as it came to her, the word 'grandfather' felt both alien and intimate. Elven suddenly felt sorry for him. An old man dying alone. An old man whose daughter had shamed him by marrying outside her race—an inferior race no less!

'*She shall find love if she opens it.*' Elven kneaded her mother's words over and over in her mind as if they were a ball of pastry dough.

In the orphanage, she was often told that she was loved. All the children were told that they were loved. It was announced daily by Director Hammond himself in the morning assembly. One would think that any child growing up in such an environment would be an expert on love. Yet Elven never quite understood it.

What is love?

If love is a feeling, is it hot or cold? If it is a sensation, is it prickly like a hedgehog or cuddly like a teddy bear? Why was it that while she was 'surrounded' by love, she couldn't see, smell, or touch it?

Suddenly, an unpleasant thought interrupted her reverie. Was someone playing an elaborate joke on her? She briefly considered the bullies in the orphanage, but there was no way they could have posted this parcel. And even if they knew someone on the outside, why go through the trouble of buying such an expensive-looking box just to mock her?

Elven doubled over, pushing her forehead against the damp grass as tears welled up in her eyes. What was she to make of this letter, with its honest yet cruel voice? A dying man's confession? An attempt to drive her mad with an unsolvable puzzle? Reflexively, she stroked the extra stump on her left hand with her thumb, as she always did when in need of comfort. But now the familiar gesture felt grotesque. Was her deformity really God's punishment for her grandfather's sins?

'What are you doing here?' a voice rang out above her. It was Coal, still wearing his dirty apron from the kitchen.

Instinctively, Elven hid the Puzzle Box behind her as she scrambled to her feet.

'It's so unlike you to miss supper, especially when *I'm* cooking,' he continued.

'But you cook every night,' she said.

'Exactly my point.' He grinned and held out a bag of containers for her. 'Here, I saved you some of my famous mushroom and chestnut soup, with bits and pieces from supper. You wouldn't believe the amount of fresh mushrooms I found in the woods yesterday. You know the kind that has a meaty taste? It really made a diff—' He stopped, staring hard at her in the fading light. 'Elv, are you . . . crying?'

She shook her head, nodded, then wiped her eyes with the back of her hand. It was too hard to speak without breaking into tears again. Coal spotted the letter on the grass and bent to pick it up.

'Read it,' Elven said.

Coal squinted at the paper, his mouth moving as he struggled with the words.

'Native?' Coal exclaimed. 'Does that mean you're—'

'Mawoli,' Elven said. 'I'm half Mawoli.'

They fell silent at the enormity of that revelation. All her life, Elven had fought against the speculation that she was half Native. The light honey skin, the narrow almond-shaped eyes, the head of dark straight hair. She had always attributed her features to an imagined Mavarian bloodline.

Now, there was no escaping the truth. She was a half-breed. The product of a scandal.

'You mustn't tell anyone,' she whispered to Coal. 'Promise me.'

'No, of course not.' Even Coal—funny Coal, you-can't-shock-me Coal, nothing-to-fear Coal—was suddenly serious. He opened his mouth and hesitated slightly before finally saying, 'You're still Elv to me. So what if you're half—'

'Don't say it!' she cried, as if that would change the awful truth.

'At least you know that your father's alive,' Coal said.

'Do NOT talk about him!' She glared at Coal. 'If there's anything worse than having a good-for-nothing for a father, it's having a good-for-nothing Mawoli for a father.'

Coal shrugged and went back to the letter. Several times, he had to stop and ask her to decipher some of the longer words for him. Finally, when he came to the end, Elven handed him the Puzzle Box. He held it up to the light and let out a whistle.

'A family treasure! What's inside?'

'I don't know.' Elven sighed. 'I'm not even sure I can open it.'

'Why not?' Coal asked, examining the Puzzle Box.

'Because my grandfather tried for twelve years and failed.'

'There must be someone who can,' said Coal. 'What about the person who made this box? I bet he'll know how to open it.'

'But where in the world is he?' asked Elven.

'Easy-peasy.' Coal pointed to the seal. 'The answer's right here.'

4

An Adventure Beckons

'This inverted v is Mount Armora,' Coal explained. 'See that little kink at the tip of the v? It's unmistakable.'

Elven's heart gave a quick flutter but she steadied herself. She knew Mount Armora—everyone did. It was the tallest mountain for miles around. But she found it hard to believe that a box so intricate could be made on a mountain.

'It could be just an inverted v that's badly written . . .' She held the box up against the sky, trying to catch the light of the setting sun. There seemed to be an oval—the size of a barley grain—right under the inverted v. And below it, someone had scratched a squiggly line. 'Is that the letter o?'

Coal did not answer but pushed open the shed door. Elven glanced around before following him inside. Large cardboard boxes were stacked against the long wall opposite the door while steel racks packed with junk lined the one on the right. A dusty table cluttered with tools stood to the left. Under the dim orange light,

Coal rummaged through the contents of its top drawer and produced a magnifying glass.

'It's not an o,' he said as he steadied the glass above the box. 'It's an acorn. Wait, what's that below?'

They let out a gasp as the squiggle came into focus.

Armora

'By God, you're right!' Elven sprang up, nearly tripping over a fallen rake. Suddenly for the first time today, she felt hopeful. She might have lost out on the scholarship, but here was her once-in-a-lifetime chance at finding love—or whatever her mother meant by that.

She turned to Coal, her eyes burning with excitement. 'Now that we know where the box maker is, we have to leave immediately!'

'Leave?' Coal's eyebrows shot up.

'Why? Is it too far to walk?'

'Blimey!' Coal opened his mouth in mock horror. 'You can't just take off, silly. Armora is a town at the foot of Mount Armora. It'll take days to walk there. Why can't you just write to him?'

'I don't want to write.' Elven clasped the Puzzle Box to her chest. 'I want to be there to see him open the box.'

For once, Coal was speechless.

'Come with me, please?' Elven begged. 'It'll be a great, big adventure!'

'I can't just run off.' Coal scrunched up his face. 'I only have a few more months to go.'

'Precisely. What difference does it make?'

'You don't understand. The director's promised to write me a reference. Without his letter, nobody'll hire me. Then, what'll I do?'

Elven's fingers tightened over the Puzzle Box.

'You were the one who smuggled me the box. You said not to let them take it away from me!'

'Uh-huh—'

'This place is going to change me,' Elven cried. 'So what if I bake the best pastries in all of Kalimasia? All the baking in the world's never going to be enough.'

After what seemed like eternity, Coal let out a sigh. 'I can see why you have to go, but you don't have to decide now, right?'

Elven shook her head. 'I have to leave tonight. Don't forget they're coming to mend that stretch of damaged fence tomorrow.'

A deep frown cut across Coal's forehead. Elven wasn't sure if it was because he was distraught by her decision or because he would no longer be able to slip out into the woods.

'Guess that's the end of my wild mushrooms recipes,' Coal said, glancing ruefully at the container of soup.

'Or at least until the next storm,' Elven said.

Coal perked up. 'Come,' he said, 'give me a hand.'

He walked to the back of the shed and began moving the stack of boxes along the wall. Elven followed suit, although she had no idea what they were doing.

'Is there a secret tunnel in here?' she asked.

'That would be most helpful, wouldn't it?' Coal muttered. He pushed past a few wooden crates and disappeared into the gap between. There was a rustling of heavy fabric before Coal reappeared with a shiny red bicycle, his chest all puffed out.

'It's beautiful, isn't it?' Coal said with a big grin. 'I found it in the woods all rusty and twisted out of shape. Been working on it for a year now.' He held out the bicycle to Elven. 'This is a much more practical option for your escape, I think.'

Elven stared back, speechless. How in the world did Coal get his hands on a bicycle? 'Oh, but I—'

The smile on Coal's face vanished. 'Don't you like it?'

'I do, I do!' Elven wasn't sure whether to laugh or cry. 'But I can't possibly take this from you!'

'Yes, you can,' Coal insisted.

'It's too nice—'

'Stop arguing for once!'

'Fine. Then, tell me why you can't leave with me.'

'I've told you!' he replied, his eyes flashing. 'Please, let's not—'

The toll of the courtyard bell sliced through his sentence. It signalled that the caretakers would soon start rounding everyone up for the nightly headcount.

Without another word, Coal retrieved a canvas bag from one of the boxes and stuffed it into the bicycle's basket. 'There's a map, a compass, candles, matches, a jar of pickled tomatoes, and an empty flask in here,' he said. 'If you head north along the main road, you'll reach Armora soon enough. And don't forget the supper.'

'Is this goodbye, then?' Elven asked, regretting their quarrel.

'No.' Coal reached his arms around her waist and untied her apron in a swift tug. 'You don't need this where you're going,' he said, tossing it aside.

Elven's ears burned a bright red. Her heart was thumping so hard she felt sure he was deafened by the sound of it.

'Look, I'll join you when I turn sixteen,' he said. 'I promise.'

Elven nodded reluctantly and took over the bicycle. The metal handlebars felt smooth and cool under her hot palms. She knew she should be happy. But for some reason, she felt shredded by his decisiveness.

Coal peeked outside the shed, and the two of them hurried towards the fence in silence. Fortunately, the ground was hard and dry. There would be no tracks to get him into trouble.

When they reached the chain-link fence, Coal lifted up the loose, three-foot-tall flap so she could just push the bicycle under. They stood for a moment, the piece of metal awkwardly hanging between them.

'I guess this is it,' Coal said with a wry smile.

Elven got down on her belly and slid under the fence. The grass on the other side was overgrown with wild flowers. Small white blossoms appeared luminous even in the fading light. The earth smelled sweet and fresh. Her first whiff of freedom.

When she looked up, Coal's silhouette had merged into the encroaching shadows.

5

The Town of Love and Gold

The last forty hours had been exhausting. Elven had cycled for most part of the first night, simply afraid to keep still lest the orphanage staff hunt her down. It was only when she saw a signboard indicating the county line that she allowed herself a short nap in the morning.

When she awoke, the sun was already high in the sky. She drank the rest of her mushroom soup and pushed on until the dirt road led her into a valley. At dusk, she set up a bed of branches, twigs, and leaves under a tree. There, she fell asleep, dreaming about her mother.

The next morning, after waking and filling her flask with spring water, she was on the road again, cycling out of the valley with only quick stops for small bites of her ration.

As Elven pedalled up the steep terrain, her aching calf muscles burned as if to the bones. Groaning, she raised her bum off the hard leather seat, hoping to ease the soreness. It was as helpful as applying salt to a wound, but there could be no letting up, not unless she wanted to get caught.

She was nearly at the top of the hill.

Hang on, she told herself. *You're almost there.*

She gave it all she had. The bicycle flew up the dirt trail and trundled to a stop on a rocky clearing. Immediately, Elven got off and lay down on the ground. It felt so good to be still. Her body, though used to physical hardship, felt beaten and abused. Yet, she had also never felt more alive.

When Elven finally sat up, she noticed a wooden signboard about ten feet away. Rubbing her eyes, she walked towards it, reading and re-reading the neat white letters painted on a background of ivy green.

Welcome to Armora, Town of Love and Gold.

In the distance, a mountain rose up like an inverted v. The emerald cone with the small dip at the summit was strangely familiar. Had she seen it before?

She inhaled sharply. Of course! It was Mount Armora—the symbol carved on the bottom of the Puzzle Box!

Between the hill and the mountain lay a sea of pastel-hued houses topped with roofs in shades of orange. Armora looked neat and picturesque. Like a toy Christmas town display someone had donated to the orphanage, only without the snow.

There was a wooden box attached below the signboard. From it, Elven fished out a map printed on rough paper. Armora was cut up into five segments by roads converging north onto a semi-circular plaza. Above the plaza, the mapmaker had drawn in clusters of trees and wavy lines to represent the contours of Mount Armora. At the left bottom corner was a boxed legend listing seven attractions, none of which looked particularly interesting. A little hut at the corner of the plaza caught her eye. The words next to it read in bold: Tourist Information. *That'll be your best bet*, she could almost hear Coal say.

Watching the clouds drift by overhead, she thought about her best friend. Without his help, she would never have made it this far. But what if she had gotten him into trouble? What if the caretakers were punishing him so he would divulge her whereabouts? She ran back to her bicycle and turned it back along the trail.

No! She stopped herself. She would only let Coal down if she returned with nothing to show. She had to uncover the secret of the Puzzle Box, find love—as unlovable as she was—and share it with him. A long time ago, Mr Singh had told her a story about a genie who granted three wishes to the person who freed him from an oil lamp. What if there was a genie in the Puzzle Box? What if this genie could find a family who would adopt both her *and* Coal? Maybe it could even lighten her skin tone and make her look less Native. Maybe it could make her eleventh finger disappear. Her head grew dizzy at the endless possibilities. No, she couldn't go back. She was beyond the point of no return. Tucking the map into her pocket, she mounted her bicycle and headed out of the clearing.

The bicycle accelerated down the windy dirt trail, picking up so much speed she feared she was going to get flung off the hill. Finally, the steep, dusty road gave way to stretches of flat, jagged stones. At the bottom of the hill was a gurgling creek. Elven followed its curve until she came to a timber bridge, which looked more green than brown because of the moss growing on it.

Once across the water, the wild lines of nature soon gave way to a wide plain littered with abandoned barns. Before long, houses began appearing on the horizon. The bungalows at the edge of town were large, with several gardens boasting stone sculptures and fountains. These soon gave way to neat rows of terraced houses with balconies and spiral staircases.

By the time Elven pedalled past these homes, the unpaved road had widened into a cobblestone street. On either side, baskets of flowers hung from neat rows of cast iron street lamps. In a small, gated park, a group of women were pruning bougainvillea bushes while their children ran around playing catch. Then came a row of shops selling clothes, shoes, and fancy hats decorated with peacock feathers and sprays of pearls.

Taking in the sweet scent of baked goods from the open door of a bakery, Elven felt, for the first time in days, comforted by the familiar. There were a good many people about and none of them looked like they were in any hurry. Smiles and friendly nods greeted her as she rode up the spotless streets. She had never seen so many happy adults all in one place.

Passing under an arch, she suddenly found herself in the town plaza. Elven braked to a stop, astounded by the grandeur of it all. About thirty feet in front of her, water danced in exuberant splashes from a marble fountain carved with carps and dragons. Behind her, two- and three-storeyed buildings ran along the edge of the semi-circular open space, fronted by cafes and shops. On the opposite end, a church with a bell tower stood proudly, framed by brick buildings on either side. And, in the background, rising above the crown of trees was Mount Armora in all its splendour.

How could she ever go back to the orphanage after she had seen this?

Unsure if she was allowed to ride across the expensive-looking granite pavers, Elven got off her bicycle and pushed it towards the Tourist Information hut located a few yards before the church. A flock of pigeons milled about the middle of the plaza, barely paying attention to her as she walked by.

Elven parked her bicycle next to the hut and approached the window. There was a man reading a book with his feet propped up against the counter. Elven coughed.

'Oh, hello!' the man said, putting his feet down in a hurry. 'Welcome! Are you alone?'

'Erm . . . no. I'm here with my—' Elven fingered the Puzzle Box in her pocket '—my grandfather.'

The man introduced himself as the tourism manager of Armora. 'Would you like to hear about our attractions?'

'Actually, I'm—'

'None of the boring museums for you?' the tourism manager interrupted.

'Actually, I'm hoping to buy a puzzle box.'

'Oh? A Takuno admirer?' the tourism manager asked. 'We don't get many of them coming here these days.'

'Takuno?'

'Yes, Armora's adopted son from the North and Kalimasia's most famous puzzle box maker.'

'Right, of course!' Elven said hurriedly. 'Where can I find him?'

'You can't. Master Takuno closed his workshop and moved away a few years ago.'

'Moved away?' Elven blinked. She felt she must have heard wrong. 'But where did he go?' Her voice came out as a croak.

'I'm afraid I don't know,' the tourism manager said with a sympathetic smile. 'If I did, I would surely announce it to all the puzzle box aficionados around the country.'

Elven's fingers gripped the ledge of the counter. 'Is there another maker in Armora? Someone like Master Takuno?' If there was another Master in Armora, maybe he could help her open her box.

'Oh no . . . We don't have any other makers here. Master Takuno was the first, the last, and the only.'

'What about the neighbouring towns or villages at the foot of the mountain?'

'I doubt it.' The tourism manager scratched his beard. 'There's no one quite like him in the whole of Kalimasia.'

In that case, her box must have been made by him.

'Look,' continued the tourism manager, 'if you aren't picky, the gift shop on Main Street sells puzzle boxes too.'

Elven perked up. 'They do?'

'Well . . . if you're expecting something as intricate as a Takuno, you'll be disappointed.' The tourism manager leaned over and continued in a conspiratorial whisper, 'The ones in the shop are poor replicas made in a factory. My nephew has one and the Key doesn't even work—'

'What key?' Elven did not remember seeing a key in the package. Had it slipped out of the envelope? Or had she absent-mindedly thrown it away with the parcel wrapping? 'How big is it?'

The man laughed and slapped the counter. 'Not *that* kind of key! You see, every puzzle box contains a coded message from the giver to the receiver. In Armora, we call it the Key.'

'I don't understand . . . So, what if you lose this Key?'

'You can't lose it, love!' the tourism manager exclaimed. 'This is not a physical key I'm talking about. This Key is a secret word or phrase.' He leaned against the counter with a smile. 'The puzzle box is a token of love, a way to tell someone *why* you love them. For example, if a man falls in love with a beautiful woman, he might give her a puzzle box coded with the word "BEAUTY". Or if he loves her truthful nature, he might code it with the word "HONESTY". Now, here comes the fun part. When the woman receives the box, the word is scrambled. In order to open the box, she has to push the tiles around until she unscrambles the Key. Once the letters fall into place, presto! The box springs open with a single touch, revealing the treasure inside.'

'A treasure?' Elven's eyes grew wide. Could there possibly be a jewel or a gold coin inside her box? A family heirloom?

'I'm speaking figuratively, of course. It could be anything from a musty old hankie to a baby tooth, haha.'

'Oh,' Elven said, forcing a smile.

Above them, the clock tower struck twelve.

'Ah, lunchtime!' The tourism manager took off his blazer and hung it over his chair. 'Oh well, I'm sorry that you'll leave empty-handed. But Armora has so much to offer. I hope you'll at least explore the town before you go.' He beamed at her brightly. 'Perhaps there's something else I can help you with?'

Elven bit her lips. 'Is there anyone who can tell me where Master Takuno went?'

'You don't give up, do you?' the tourism manager said. 'Try the Heritage Museum across the plaza. Maybe they'll be able to help you.'

Elven thanked him and pushed her bicycle slowly across the granite pavers. When she was behind the fountain, she stopped and slipped the box out of her pocket.

YOU ARE MINE.

The words said it perfectly. Her mother loved her because Elven was her daughter. This had to be her Key. But why wouldn't the box open?

6

A Reason for Love

The Heritage Museum was closed for lunch. At the pub a few doors away, groups of men in suits and ties were having their meal at the tables outside, under the shade of a large birch tree. As the aroma of their steaks and potatoes wafted over, Elven's stomach rumbled.

Sitting down on a stone step, she opened her satchel and drank the last drop of water from her bottle. That did not make her full, so she opened the box that held her rations. There was only half a jar of pickled tomatoes left, a hunk of bread that looked slightly greenish at the edges, a small yam, and a rib bone.

After a moment's hesitation, she gobbled up the bread, only to be assaulted by an immediate sense of regret.

What have I done? Not only had she finished all her water but she had also almost eaten up everything. And she was still hungry. Unbearably hungry. It was as if all the water and bread had fallen into the quicksand that lined her stomach walls, leaving her actual stomach as empty as before.

Suddenly she felt a tap on her shoulder. Elven turned her head and saw a boy staring at her.

'Want a dinner roll?' he asked, holding out the softest, most aromatic round roll in his hand.

Elven swallowed, unable to take her eyes off the layer of fresh butter glistening under the sun. She stood up and blurted out a profusion of thanks. But just as she reached forward, the boy clamped his chubby fingers close.

'Not so fast,' he said, narrowing his large eyes, which no longer looked so cherubic. 'Before you take the roll, you have to tell me who you are and why you're here.'

The boy was perhaps two or three years younger, but right now, his three-piece suit and intense stare made him seem more like a worldly adult.

Elven opened her mouth but found herself tongue-tied. In the orphanage, they were often told by the caretakers that there was no such thing as a 'free lunch'. The orphanage was a cold, hard place, and you only got what you earned. But the outside world was supposed to be different!

Her pride told her to walk away from this bait, but her legs seemed rooted to the spot. Without warning, her stomach betrayed her with a loud rumble. The boy tried to suppress a smile. Elven's dignity shrivelled up like dried leaves. All she could think of was how it would feel to sink her teeth into the soft, moist bread.

'My name is Elven,' she said, reluctantly.

'And I'm Harris,' the boy replied. 'Why are you here, Elven?'

'To look for Master Takuno, the puzzle box maker.'

'Ah, puzzle boxes,' the boy answered. 'I have one myself, an authentic Takuno.'

Elven's eyes nearly popped out of their sockets. 'You do?'

'Yes, it was a present for my seventh birthday.'

'Do you know if a Takuno Puzzle Box can be . . . faulty?' Elven asked. 'Like if some don't open even though the Key is shown?'

'Impossible! My papa says that a Takuno lasts a lifetime,' Harris scoffed. 'Why? Do you have a Puzzle Box that won't open?'

Elven paused, wondering if she could trust him. 'Not me,' she finally said. 'A friend . . . her box wouldn't open. She wanted me to help her ask Master Takuno if it's because the box is too old.'

'Too old?' Harris rolled his eyes. 'Sounds like an imitation.'

'Most certainly not,' Elven protested. 'It's got an Armora seal.'

'What if it's got a seal?' Harris said, his voice dripping with disdain. 'Anyone can fake a seal.'

Elven sank back down on the stone step, feeling like she had been slapped in the face. If the Puzzle Box wasn't handmade then perhaps the letter might be fake too.

'Are you all right?' Harris asked.

Elven squeezed her eyes shut. *Have I run away for nothing?*

'You look very pale,' Harris said.

'Go away, please.'

'Look, sorry. I was exaggerating. I'm not actually sure factory-made boxes come with seals.' Harris pressed the roll into her hand.

Elven opened her eyes. 'So, it's possible that my box . . . I mean, my friend's box . . . is a real Takuno?'

Harris gave an awkward nod. 'Maybe she just got the Key wrong. It happens, you know. When people are too sure of themselves.'

Was she too sure of herself? She had thought nothing of running away from the only home she had known, arrogantly believing that she—with her tainted Mawoli blood—could solve a puzzle her grandfather couldn't.

'Besides, how difficult can it be to find a reason for love?' Harris chattered on. 'My parents' reasons are always about me being strong and good at sports—'

'I have to go,' Elven said, standing up.

'Wait! Do you have to?' Harris protested. 'There aren't that many kids who can hold a decent conversation around here.'

Elven laughed. 'Well, I really need to find out where Master Takuno moved to.'

'Papa will know,' Harris said eagerly. 'He's very well-connected. Will you stay a while longer if I get the address?'

'It's a deal!'

Signalling for her to stay put, Harris ran up to the group of men. Elven stuffed the roll into her mouth as she watched the boy tug on one of the men's sleeves.

'Papa, what is Master Takuno's new address?' Harris asked.

'Takuno?' his father asked. 'What's he got to do with you?'

'I need it for a friend.'

'Not now.' His father waved his hand irritably, like he was swatting away a fly. 'The little bugger's just trying to get our attention,' he added to his friends.

'You never take me seriously!' Harris brought his fist down on the table with such force that the pale-coloured ale quivered in their glasses and threatened to spill out.

The adults swore and lunged forward to rescue their drinks. Harris' father roared in displeasure. Grabbing his son by the lapels of his shirt, he shook him so hard that Harris' teeth rattled like a wind vane in a storm.

'Look here, boy,' he shouted as he dragged his son, kicking and screaming away from the table. 'If you don't shut up this instant, I will send you to the mountain witch!' His father loosened his grip and Harris crumbled to the ground, panting. At the sight of this, Elven realized that she, too, needed to breathe.

'Trouble with your son, Mr Wyn?'

A tall man rose from the next table. He was built like a beanpole, with thin hair parted down the middle. The conversation around the tables fell to a whisper.

'Mayor Moore, I hadn't realized you were here . . .' Harris' father stuttered. He had turned a vivid shade of red from the neck up. 'You know kids, they go berserk sometimes.'

'Children need to understand,' the mayor said, walking over with a slow, menacing gait, 'who the boss is. Those who don't understand—or refuse to understand—should be guided with a firm hand.'

He bent down and pointed his index finger straight at Harris' nose.

'Son, when you behave in an irrational manner, you disturb the peace in our beautiful plaza,' he said coldly.

'Please accept my apologies,' Harris' father said hoarsely. 'I will bring him home right away.'

'No, no. Not right away,' the mayor insisted with an ironic smile. 'Finish your drink, old chap. You're the boss, remember?'

'Yes, sir.' Harris' father gave a nervous laugh. 'Of course.'

The mayor nodded and went back to his table. Harris' father shot his son a warning look before rejoining his friends.

'Good heavens!' exclaimed Elven, running over to help Harris up.

'That didn't go as planned,' Harris sniffed. 'No thanks to the mayor.' After staring moodily at his father's back, he picked himself up—not without wincing—and dusted his suit.

'Everyone looks pretty scared of the mayor,' Elven said, hoping to make Harris feel less self-conscious.

'Oh, you don't want to offend him,' he assured her. 'Mayor Moore's a regular guest on the capital radio station. If he doesn't like you, he bad-mouths you on air and there goes your reputation.'

Elven nodded, stealing another look at the mayor. No wonder his voice sounded familiar. She must have heard him on one of the radio shows Cook listened to in the kitchen.

'I hate it when Papa threatens me with the witch,' Harris mumbled.

'Is there really a mountain witch?' Elven asked, hoping her question didn't sound too stupid.

Harris hooted in disbelief. 'Haven't you heard? Naughty children are sent to live with her as their punishment.' He pointed to Mount Armora. 'Once you're imprisoned, you're either turned into a black cat or made to work all day and night digging out gold from Mount Armora. The little sleep you'll get is in the pre-dawn hours when the witch goes off to gather herbs for her spells. Even that's in a cage!'

'So, when do these children get to come home?'

'They don't,' Harris said in a low voice. 'Not until they're old and weak, and their parents have forgotten all about them.' He stole a glance at his father's back. 'And then, there are the special ones who never return. The ones she keeps as her sustenance!'

Elven let out a shriek. 'You m-mean she feeds on them?'

'But not in the way you think. Oh no,' Harris countered, wagging his index finger, 'this is not some silly fairy tale like "Jack and the Beanstalk" where a stupid giant catches and eats boys. This is real and it's happening right here.' Harris narrowed his eyes. 'The witch sustains her black magic by feeding on the blood of a special breed of children. Every night, she makes a cut on their arms and drinks their blood. Not to the extent that they bleed out and die, mind you. But enough for her to retain her youth and power.'

Despite the warmth of the sun, Elven shivered. 'What's so special about these children?'

'They're half Mawoli,' Harris whispered.

'No way!' Was Harris taking the piss out of her? Maybe he had noticed her skin tone and put one and one together.

'We don't know why only half-Mawoli children will do,' he continued, seemingly oblivious to her agitation. 'Some say something special happens when the blood of the lowest race gets mixed in with the elites. Something that attracts evil—'

A stern shout from Harris' father interrupted him. They turned and saw Mr Wyn eying them with disapproval.

'Harris, we're leaving,' Mr Wyn growled.

'Come visit me later?' Harris asked as he grabbed his bicycle. 'I can bring you to Master Takuno's workshop. Just look for me in the small blue house next to the library—'

'Get over here now!' Mr Wyn exploded.

Harris jumped onto his bicycle and flew towards his father.

'Son, I don't want you mixing with those types,' Mr Wyn said as he cast a dirty look at Elven.

Elven felt like she had just been punched. All around, the eyes of the diners were burning through her, judging her every move. Shaking, she held her satchel against her chest, taking care to hide her eleventh finger with her right palm.

I will not run. I will not run, she repeated to herself. *I did nothing wrong.*

She forced herself to walk away with her head held high.

Just then, a man in a fedora hat and a crumpled brown suit strolled up to the Heritage Museum. Taking out a key from his pocket, he fumbled with the lock for a moment before disappearing behind the timber doors.

The man's presence jolted Elven out of her humiliation, and she knew in no uncertain terms what she had to do.

I don't care if he throws me out, Elven thought as she hurried over. *I need to open my Puzzle Box.*

7

Takuno's Trick

When Elven pulled open the heavy door of the Heritage Museum, she found the man had disappeared. Inside the empty rectangular room, wood-trimmed glass cases were lined up neatly along the dark green walls decorated with black-and-white photographs. In the middle, a chandelier hung above a round table, casting a faint glow on the display of odd-shaped rock samples. Elven had only ever seen a chandelier in the orphanage's Staff Wing and it was nothing compared to this gigantic crown of twisted brass and glass droplets.

She made her way towards the desk at the back of the room, careful to give the heavy light fixture a wide berth. On the left wall was a large oil painting showing a group of dirty-looking men crouching next to a creek. One of the men held a round metal pan in his hands and looked as if he was instructing the others how to use it. A small white card below the painting read: *Miners panning for gold.*

The desk was cluttered with stacks of leather-bound books. Elven poked about the thick volumes, hoping to find a bell to ring. There wasn't one but she left plenty of guilty fingerprints on the dusty covers.

Suddenly, a door to the side opened and an old man stepped out with a loaded tray.

'Aimee?' His teacup and plate hit the hardwood floor, shattering into pieces.

Elven glanced at the mess and then around them. There was nobody else in the museum. Surely 'Aimee' was not an obscure slang for half Natives like her?

'Is that you, Aimee?' the old man repeated, squinting right at her.

'I'm not Aimee,' she said.

The old man blinked.

'Yes, of course, the eyes are different,' he said, brushing his white hair back in embarrassment. 'I apologize, my dear. I was confused.' There was an awkward silence as he wiped his hands clumsily on his trousers. 'You look so much like her.' He stepped over the broken ceramic pieces, shaking his head. 'But of course, she would be much older by now.'

'Can I help you clean up?' Elven offered.

'No, no, leave it.'

Elven stiffened. Maybe he just didn't like half Natives touching his things.

He reached over to the desk where his gold-rimmed glasses lay and put them on with a sigh. 'Don't worry, dear,' he said, as if sensing Elven's discomfort. 'It's not like we're going to have tons of visitors streaming through the door.' His eyes crinkled up in a smile. 'I'm Mr Long. What's your name?'

'Elven . . .' she replied, glancing at the soggy hog jerky on the floor. 'Elven Bayou.'

'Ah, you're of Mavarian descent, then,' Mr Long said.

'Y-yes,' Elven stammered. She hadn't meant to lie, but somehow the old caretaker's surname popped out of her mouth just like that.

'Can I interest you in our latest exhibit, love? We have just received a donation of gold nuggets from the late County Clerk.'

Elven's eyes widened. '*Real* gold?'

'We only display the real thing,' Mr Long said with a chuckle so genuine that Elven found herself joining in. 'Are you here to find out more about Armora's gold mining history?'

'Actually, I'm here to see the puzzle boxes.'

'Ah, of course.' Mr Long beamed and gestured her over to the glass case in the corner. 'These were made right here in Armora, by the world-renowned Master Takuno.'

Elven could not help but gape at the intricate-looking boxes in the display case. They were much larger than the one she had. The biggest was roughly the size of a loaf of bread, and the smallest was still at least two inches longer than hers. Yet, what identified them as puzzle boxes were the Keys. All across the top surfaces were square wooden tiles that were either blank or marked with letters. All were scrambled. The sides, on the other hand, were inlaid with wooden pieces of different shapes and colours to create mosaics of patterns.

'People ask me what the difference is between a handmade puzzle box and a factory-made one. The answer is obvious once you see the former. Look at the design. Intricate, isn't it?' Mr Long beamed like a proud father. 'See this box here with the shimmering effect? Master Takuno used ten types of wood to get that gradation of colours. He laid them by hand, piece by piece.'

'Do you know their Keys?' Elven asked, pressing her nose against the glass case. 'Do they really open up with the right word?'

'Why yes, it's the most marvellous feeling to unlock a puzzle box.'

'Can I try?' The words tumbled out of her mouth before she could stop them. She held her breath. Would Mr Long be offended?

Mr Long hesitated for a moment before a smile crept across his wrinkled face. 'Well, all right,' he said with a wink. 'But you must be very careful.' He unlocked the case, retrieved a square puzzle box and placed it on top of the glass. 'This one is almost unlocked. Now, what word can you make with E, P, A, C, E?'

Elven stared hard at the tiles, but her mind drew a blank. She shook her head, her cheeks burning. How could she hope to open her mother's box if she couldn't even figure out a simple five-letter Key?

'Don't overthink it,' Mr Long said kindly. 'Just a single letter and everything changes. Here's a clue for you: tranquillity. When your mind is tranquil, the answer reveals itself.'

Elven closed her eyes and took a deep breath. Tranquillity. When was the last time she felt that? In the woods, picking mushrooms with Coal . . . Late at night, when everyone was asleep . . .

Her eyes shot open. 'Is it PEACE?'

'Try it,' Mr Long suggested with a twinkle in his eyes. 'Let your fingers guide the tiles. Do not think about your fingers guiding the tiles. Simply let them.'

Elven moved the first letter E up and above P. Then, pushing P to the left, she dropped E down on the empty spot.

'Excellent, my dear.' Mr Long reached out and gave the side of the box a slight push with this thumb. With a click, the top surface of the box popped open.

'My goodness!' exclaimed Elven. 'It worked!'

'The show's not over.' Mr Long laughed, putting the lid on the glass case. 'See what happens when I apply pressure here.' He tapped on the edges in quick succession and, out of nowhere, splits began to appear across the four corners. 'Ready?' Mr Long asked, peering above his glasses.

Elven nodded eagerly. The old man tapped one final time on the bottom. Before Elven could let out her breath, the box had collapsed into a pile of interlocking pieces.

'This is an early version of the self-opening puzzle box.' Mr Long laid out the six separate pieces side by side. 'The later versions have fewer pressure points so they give the impression of opening up automatically.

Superstitious folks think it's magic, but we know that it is craftsmanship and engineering.'

The old man's gentle manners reminded Elven of her teacher, Mr Singh. If Mr Long suspected that she was a half Mawoli, he did not seem to mind.

Yes, she thought, *I can trust him.*

'Mr Long,' Elven asked, looking up at the sprightly old man. 'Is it possible that a puzzle box doesn't open up even when you've discovered its Key?'

'Not to my knowledge, love.' He laughed and patted her lightly on the head.

Elven fished out the Puzzle Box from her pocket. 'This doesn't.'

Mr Long's eyes lit up. 'My goodness,' he said, leaning in for a closer look. 'This must be the smallest Puzzle Box I've ever seen. And one of the loveliest Keys too.'

Elven turned the box around so that he could see the seal at the bottom.

'Is this a real Takuno?' she asked.

Mr Long opened a felt-lined drawer under the glass case and retrieved a magnifying glass.

'Yes, it is,' Mr Long said, peering at the seal. 'No one else carves an acorn with such care as Master Takuno.'

'Not even the machines in the factory?'

Mr Long gave a wry smile. 'Intricate detailing is something machines are incapable of, at least for now. And look at the colour gradation created by the careful selection of teak, cherry, and maple. This is Master Takuno at his best.'

Elven heaved a sigh of relief. 'But why doesn't it open?' she asked.

'May I?'

'Please.'

Mr Long took the box from Elven and turned it around in his palm. 'Well, you've got the Key,' he said, 'so it should be quite simple.' He pressed the side panel with his thumb.

Elven held her breath. Would this be the moment when her new life began? Perhaps the box was a test her grandfather had set for her. If she passed, he would adopt her back into the family. Or perhaps it contained information about her father—who maybe wasn't Mawoli after all—and a way to reunite with him. Or maybe . . .

Mr Long shook the box, rattling the object inside. He pressed again, this time harder. The box did not budge.

'I don't understand,' Mr Long said, scratching his beard. 'It should open if the Key shows.'

'Maybe the joints are faulty?' she offered.

'Heavens no! This is not your cheap factory imitation!' Mr Long insisted. He peered at the Puzzle Box for a long time before letting out a sigh of either regret or admiration. 'We're missing something.'

'What do you mean?'

'I have heard that some puzzle boxes are especially hard to open,' Mr Long said with a frown. 'Not only do the Keys need to be right, the letters themselves need to be put in place in the correct sequence, tile by tile.'

Elven's eyes widened in excitement. 'Are you saying I just need to try reassembling the Key in different sequences until one works?'

'Does nothing deter you, dear?' Mr Long's intense expression melted into open admiration. 'Perhaps it might work. Perhaps not. Master Takuno is fond of tricks, you know.'

At his words, Elven suddenly remembered why she had come. 'Do you know where Master Takuno has gone, sir?'

'I believe he's in a village next to Bowler Hat Lake,' Mr Long said, returning the Puzzle Box back to her.

'Where's that?'

'It's on the other side of Mount Armora, to the north.'

'Can you cycle there?'

Mr Long looked taken aback. 'I suppose so. Although heaven knows why anyone would do that.'

'There is a road, then? Across the mountain?'

'Yes, an old road . . . but nobody uses it any more, not after the railway was built.'

'A train to Bowler Hat Lake!' cried Elven. 'That'll be so much faster!' Then, her face fell. 'Oh, but there's no way I can afford a ticket . . . I guess it's the mountain road, then.'

The old man's thick brows furrowed slightly. 'Surely you're not thinking of crossing Mount Armora by yourself? It's dangerous, even in summer.'

Because of the mountain witch?

'Besides,' Mr Long continued, 'Takuno's become a recluse in old age. Even if you get there, he may not see you. You're better off working on the Puzzle Box yourself.'

'But it could take months—or decades—without his help!' Elven gripped the box in her hand and straightened her back. 'I know the odds are against me,' she said, looking Mr Long in the eye. 'But I don't have a choice.'

8

Mama Monga

With the map that Mr Long had drawn for her, Elven made her way to the library, which was next to Harris' house. The 'small blue house' that the boy had described was anything but small. In fact, it was a mansion with a front lawn twice the size of the orphanage dining hall. A stone pavement lined with pink and white bougainvillea cut through the grass, leading up to a semi-circular overhang supported by four classical columns. Harris was sitting underneath it reading a book. She shouted his name and, recognizing her immediately, he came running with a big grin.

'I thought you weren't coming!' he exclaimed. 'Want to play?'

'Actually, could you show me where Master Takuno's workshop is?' Elven asked, after a moment's hesitation. 'You said you could get me in . . .'

Harris frowned, as if regretting his promise. 'I suppose there's no harm if it's just a quick look . . .'

'I just want to find a clue to unlock my Puzzle Box. I'll be out in no time, I promise!'

Harris nodded and gestured for her to follow. They headed down a wide avenue before turning onto the smaller, more deserted Cradle Street. In contrast to the pristine streets Elven had previously associated with Armora, this one looked like it had seen better days. The weather-beaten huts here were also much more spread out, and many looked like they were in a state of disrepair. Elven and Harris weaved their way through tall and unruly weeds growing out of the pavement cracks, careful to avoid twisting their ankles in potholes the size of melons.

'Are we still in Armora?' Elven asked. Above them, a bird let out a forlorn trill.

'Of course,' Harris said. 'But not many people come to the neighbourhood of Alluvium, especially since Master Takuno is no longer here.'

A creaking sound interrupted their conversation. In the distance, a lone vendor was moving a pushcart down the street. When the vendor saw them staring, she stopped and rang her handbell meaningfully. 'Get your sticky yam balls! Sweet or salty, take your pick! Colours of the rainbow, all you can eat!'

'Oh my goodness!' Harris exclaimed. Without a moment's hesitation, he took off down the road towards the pushcart. Elven heard him holler as she ran after him, 'Mama Monga! Recognize me, Mama Monga?'

The vendor gave a cheerful wave. She was a pyramid of a woman, with rotund thighs and a barrel-like waist but curiously narrow shoulders. Her hair was shiny and black like mussel shells, looped in a braid around her head.

'Why don't you go to the library any more?' Harris asked in a slightly accusing tone.

'My spine's no good, Master Harris. Can't go that far no more.' Mama Monga pounded her shoulders with her fist, causing her entire torso to wobble like a mound of jelly. 'It's just the plaza and Alluvium for me these days.'

'Pfft!' Harris crossed his arms and made a sulky face.

'I'm here now, ain't I?' Mama Monga said in a placating voice. 'I've got the crispy seaweed one you like but tell me, what catches your fancy today?'

'Have you ever eaten a sticky yam ball?' Harris asked, turning to Elven with a grin.

Elven shook her head to say no.

'Crikey! It's the best thing in the world!' Harris exclaimed. 'Let's get one before we go in.'

'Go in where?' Elven asked, confused.

Harris pointed to the brick house standing across the street from the cart. It was a squat building with a clay tile roof fronted by flowering shrubs. On its front door was a wooden sign carved with the unmistakable seal that Elven had come to know well—the inverted v of Mount Armora above an acorn. Below it were the words 'Takuno's Puzzle Boxes. Since 1897.' engraved in gold.

'The workshop!' Elven gasped. 'I can't believe I'm actually here.'

'Oh, you'd better,' Harris said, 'because we're about to enter without permission. Now, hurry up and pick out a yam ball. I need something to calm my nerves.'

At that, Mama Monga whipped open the wooden doors of her display case, revealing three rows of sticky yam balls. They were big, each the size of a grown man's fist. Some had nuts in them, others sparkled with chocolate buttons, marzipan flowers, and bits of star-shaped toffees.

Scanning the rows of shimmering balls, Elven's eyes settled on a rainbow-coloured one drizzled with dark chocolate and dusted in gold. 'Royal Escapade', the label read. Elven reached up, fingers barely grazing the yam ball when Mama Monga stuck out her palm.

'That'll be seven cents,' she said.

'Seven cents!' Elven exclaimed.

'But the sign says six!' Harris protested.

'Yes, Master Harris, it is six cents for the sticky yam ball.' Mama Monga bent her knees and brought her brown fleshy face close to his. 'But you got to pay me an extra cent to keep my mouth sealed when your father comes around.'

Harris groaned.

'I'll even keep a lookout for you,' Mama Monga added with a glint in her narrow eyes.

'Erm, what does your father have to do with this place?' Elven asked. She didn't relish the idea of running into Mr Wyn again.

'Papa's one of Armora's top real estate agents, and Master Takuno has asked him to sell the workshop for him.' Harris counted out seven cents from his pocket and dropped them into Mama Monga's hand. 'Nothing comes cheap with you,' he complained.

The vendor let out a grin that showed her perfectly yellow teeth and handed Elven her Royal Escapade in a paper bag. Meanwhile, Harris had already crossed the street and was rummaging beneath a large shrub bursting with bright blue flowers. Elven tucked the Royal Escapade inside her pocket and crouched down next to him. The scent of the bush was at once pungent and aromatic.

'The key is hidden below the maliaki bush,' Harris said as he ran his fingers through the gravel around the plant.

'Maliaki? Isn't that the plant used for Mawoli body painting?'

'Found it!' Harris cried, leaping up with a silver key in his hand. He inserted it in the lock and pushed the heavy door open. Then, replacing the key back under the gravel, he mysteriously added, 'Just in case.'

Elven followed Harris inside the building. The door slammed shut with a bang. Harris spun around with a scowl.

'Sshh!'

'Sorry,' Elven whispered.

The workshop felt cold and musty, with a whiff of sawdust still lingering in the air. Morning sunlight filtered through the window blinds, illuminating a large, open workspace. Three pairs of round pillars held up rectangular timber beams that ran from left to right across the ceiling. Green ivy and white saucer-like flowers had been painted creeping out from the floorboards, around the pillars, and up to the beams. The effect was that of a secret garden.

The floor itself was sparsely furnished. In the middle was a large workbench and behind it, a wooden shelf surrounded by crates. To the left of where Elven stood was a round wooden table with four chairs. The tabletop was bare except for an empty vase and a sprinkling of acorns. Elven bent forward to pick up an acorn by its textured cap, only to realize that it was carved into the table.

'Haha, you fell for that too!' Harris clapped his hands in glee. 'It's a joke he played on his clients.'

Elven's heart skipped a beat. *Is this the table where Master Takuno met with my parents?* She sat down on a chair and, closing her eyes, tried to imagine her parents hunched over the table, watching intently as the craftsman sketched out their Puzzle Box design on a piece of paper.

'Hey, wake up!' Harris said, shaking her shoulders. 'We don't have all day.'

Elven opened her eyes and turned to him. 'I wonder where we should start . . .'

'You don't know?' Harris slumped his shoulders dramatically. 'You mean you don't have a plan?'

Elven grinned sheepishly. 'I thought we'd just poke around . . .' She stood up and walked to the timber workbench on which all sorts of woodworking tools rested. There were two hand planes for smoothing wood, a mitre box and saw set, and a large chest containing various sizes of steel chisels. Hanging from the bench were a number of handsaws and metal rules. As Elven walked towards the back wall, she thought she heard a soft gurgling coming from somewhere.

'Is that the sound of water?' she asked, puzzled.

Harris grinned and skipped over to where a large water wheel sat propped up against the wall. 'Surprise!' he said, pulling up a panel in the timber floor to reveal a stream below. 'The water wheel used to sit underneath here. When the water would flow through the wheel, it would set in motion the metal disc, which would then turn the belt in a loop.' He touched the leather belt running beneath the floorboard, across the space to the ceiling level, and back. 'It used to power that monster over there,' he said, pointing to a large sanding machine through which the leather belt looped.

'How do you know this?' Elven asked.

'I got a tour when Papa commissioned my puzzle box,' Harris said, looking pleased. 'And I have a good memory, better than most kids.'

Elven walked over to the shelf and rummaged through a box of timber samples.

'We should go,' Harris said, shaking an empty wood stain can and tossing it aside. 'You don't even know what you're looking for.'

Elven stared at the three large wooden crates in front of her. She lifted one of the lids and found it filled with books and letters.

'Maybe one of these books will teach me how to open my box,' she said, rifling through the pile.

'You're not going through every single one of them, are you?' Harris said in alarm. 'It's going to take forever!'

'I'll do whatever it takes,' Elven insisted. 'And it'll be much faster if you help me.'

Harris muttered something about girls and trudged over to the crate. Together, they emptied the first crate of books, most of which were on unrelated subjects like gardening, the Northern art of silk painting, and mathematics. In the second crate, they found Master Takuno's sketches for various puzzle box designs on rice paper, notebooks documenting the price and inventory of different hardwood, as well as an address book listing timber suppliers. None of these yielded any clues because they were annotated in a mixture of English and an indecipherable northern script.

'Master Takuno was so secretive,' Harris complained as he leafed through a blue-lined notebook filled with names and dates. 'Look, he even recorded the price of his goods in this "ribbon" script!' He threw the notebook across to Elven. 'No trade secrets in here.'

Elven flipped through the sales journal, which was about fifty pages thick. Each page was divided into three columns. The first column contained dates, the second the names of customers, and—true to what Harris said—the last column had prices filled in with wriggly lines.

'Some of these names are actually in English,' Elven muttered as she stared at the entries. The shadow of an idea flitted across her mind like a butterfly.

Almost immediately, the budding thought was erased by the loud ringing of a bell.

'Sticky yam balls!' the piercing voice of Mama Monga cut through the air like a steel blade. 'Any yam balls for you, *Mr Wyn*?'

9

A Sentimental Man

'Oh no! It's Papa!' Harris exclaimed, his face the colour of rice paper. 'See, I told you to hurry.'

'We've got to hide!' Elven scanned the floor, her heart thumping so hard she felt as if she was going to keel over.

'The water wheel?' Harris asked.

'No, get in here,' Elven commanded, pushing Harris into one of the wooden crates. 'Quickly!'

She dumped a pile of paper over him, ignoring his protest, and pulled the lid shut. Then, climbing into another crate, she closed the lid on herself. Before she could even adjust her position, the door swung open.

'I could have sworn I'd locked the door last week,' an agitated voice rang out.

'Calm down, Wyn,' another man replied. 'Why are you getting so worked up?'

'That street vendor really got on my nerves, coming at me like that. I thought I'd gotten rid of her by writing to the library administration but no, she's popping up all over town like bindweed after rain.'

'If only I could convince the other town council members to ban these Mawoli hawkers. You never know what kinds of disease you could catch from their food.'

Elven gritted her teeth.

'I hope that woman hasn't stolen anything from here,' Mr Wyn grumbled.

'Nobody will want to steal these outdated woodworking tools,' the other man sneered. 'Takuno's craft is a dying art. An occupation of a bygone era. Mass production is the future, old chap. My factory churns out three hundred puzzle boxes every day. And let me tell you something. Only sixty per cent of those remain in Kalimasia. The rest get exported around the world. There is growing demand, especially in the North.'

Elven inched her head forward. So, this was the man whose factory mass produced imitation boxes. Why would he be interested in Master Takuno's workshop?

'The North? Isn't that where puzzle boxes originated?'

'You heard me right.'

She peered through the horizontal slit between the timber slats and saw Mr Wyn leaning against the workbench, his belly rippling with laughter.

'What can I say?' Mr Wyn cooed. 'You're a visionary!'

The man did not reply but walked around the workshop purposefully, examining this object and that. From what Elven could see, he was tall with long thin limbs that reminded her of a praying mantis.

'So, what do you think?' Harris' father asked.

'It's exactly as I remembered it. Well, except for this mess,' the man said, stepping over Takuno's books.

'I'm sorry about the mess,' Mr Wyn apologized. 'I've hired someone to clean up this place. But you know how unreliable those Natives can be.'

The man did not reply but picked up a hand saw hanging at the side of the workbench. 'I'm surprised he kept my saw,' he said, somewhat wistfully. 'It's got my initials carved into the handle.'

'How lovely,' Mr Wyn said.

'This place ought to stay the way it is,' the man said after a while.

'Ah, in fact the police chief thinks so too.'

'Does he?' the man replied testily.

'He was just here the other day with Mr Long. They were discussing plans to preserve the workshop as a museum.'

The man laughed coldly. 'Takuno was just a woodworker,' he said. 'Who would want to travel to this isolated location to pay homage to him?' The hand saw hit the workbench with a loud clatter.

'No, sir. Financially a museum just doesn't make sense,' agreed Mr Wyn.

'The only reason why I'm here is because I'm a sentimental man.' The man coughed and kicked aside a pile of letters. 'I've spent too many years in this workshop to see it go to someone else. This place and its memories should stay private.'

'Right,' Mr Wyn said unconvincingly. 'But I'm afraid not everyone feels the same way. I have instructions to sell to whoever comes in with a bid first.'

The tall man gave a harrumph. 'How long does it take to process the paperwork for the sale?'

'I can have it done up within a week if we sign a preliminary agreement today,' Mr Wyn replied, his voice dripping with eagerness. 'My office is not that far away.'

'Let's go, then,' the man said. 'I want the key to this place as soon as possible.'

The tall man strode out of the workshop, followed closely by Harris' father. It was not until they heard the turn of the lock that Elven popped her head out of the crate. Scurrying out, she removed the lid off Harris' hiding place and helped him to his feet.

'Impressive,' Harris said, checking the watch on his wrist. 'Papa actually closed the deal in less than twenty minutes.' He climbed out of the crate, scattering rice paper all around. 'It's not for nothing that he got featured in *The Armorian Times*.'

Elven picked her way across the piles of books and peeked out of the window. The street was empty except for the pushcart. Even Mama Monga was nowhere to be seen.

'I thought he managed the mayor very well, didn't you?' Harris prattled on. 'When I grow up—'

'The mayor!' No wonder the voice sounded familiar. Elven recalled the thin, unpleasant man who had given Harris a dressing down in the plaza and made a face. 'But why would he own a puzzle box factory?'

'You can be both a mayor and factory owner,' Harris replied matter-of-factly.

'I don't like him,' Elven said. She hunched over and, pointing her finger dramatically at Harris' nose, imitated the mayor's voice. 'Children need to understand who the boss is.'

Just as they burst out in hysterical laughter, the door flew open with a bang that, once again, prompted them to scamper for the crates. In her panic, Elven tripped over a pile of books and crashed to the floor, bringing Harris with her.

'The coast is clear!' Mama Monga announced, her massive frame barely fitting into the doorway.

'Did you have to burst in on us like that?' Harris moaned, rubbing his knees as Mama Monga gave a sheepish grin.

Elven stood up and felt her pocket. 'Argh, I just squashed our sticky yam ball.'

'I mourn your loss,' Mama Monga said, backing out of the door. 'But don't even think about asking for your money back. Business is bad enough as it is.'

'You still want to share?' Elven held out the mess to Harris.

'Ugh.' He screwed up his face as he stood up. 'Let's leave before Papa returns,' he said, heading out of the door.

Elven stood staring at the beautiful space around her. She wanted to take it all in and burn it in her memory. The smell of wood, the sound of water, and, at its heart, the workbench at which Master Takuno laboured for decades. Hundreds of people had streamed through its door, driven by the desire to commemorate their love for another human being. Now that Master Takuno had moved away, love would have to find another form. The workshop would be closed forever. Not unlike a puzzle box that had lost its Key.

A gust of wind blew in through the open door, sending the rice paper fluttering across the floor. Elven picked up the Sales Journal and stuffed it into her pocket. A souvenir from a lost age.

10

A Chance Encounter

After parting with Harris, Elven cycled to the bakery at the edge of Armora to ask for a job. But the red-faced baker behind the counter called her a thief and threatened to hold her until the police arrived. She dashed out as fast as she could.

The sun was setting when Elven finally circled back to the deserted plaza. She stopped her bicycle next to the fountain, the water for which had been turned off.

The baker knows I'm a half-breed, she thought as she dismounted.

Thieving. Lazy. Dishonest. Slow.

Those were the words the orphanage caretakers had bandied around whenever they talked about the Mawolis. She had not thought twice when she herself had used them carelessly among friends. Once, she had even refused to sit next to a Mawoli orphan to prove that she was not one of 'those people'.

How could she have been so cruel? And so blind?

Her naivety about her mixed race shocked her now. Of course, she had not been adopted. Mr Hammond didn't need to get wind of any gossip to figure out that she was half Mawoli. It was obvious!

She gazed down at the clear mirror of water and was startled to see a dirty face staring back. No wonder the baker had called her names! Look at her, with her matted nest of hair, her unwashed face. She was the caricature of a Mawoli street urchin.

Elven bent over the fountain, drank a little, and tried to clean herself as best as she could. From now on, she must keep out of the sun so her skin wouldn't get any darker. If anyone even suspected that she was half Native, she would deny it with her life. No one must know the ugly truth.

She trudged over to a wooden bench. At least it was not the monsoon season. She might be a little stiff in the morning, but she would not be soaked to her skin. She lay down on the hard planks, wincing out loud as her right ankle knocked against the cast-iron arm rest. Why hadn't she packed herself a blanket?

Pulling up her legs, she tucked herself into a little ball. She had no money, a miserable portion of food left, and nobody to ask for help. How would she ever make it to Bowler Hat Lake? Unless she could find work soon, she would have to beg the orphanage to take her back.

Yet, the thought of returning to that stonewalled prison was a cold, sharp blade in her gut. Director Hammond and Mrs Monteiro would not make life easy for her—she was sure of that. There would be hours of penitence duty, much of which would consist of the dirtiest tasks, like sweeping the chimney and scrubbing the kitchen floor. She dug her fingernails into her palms and let out a moan.

A series of loud, excited barks interrupted her self-pity. In the fading light, a large dog dashed out from behind the Tourist Information hut, its leash whipping up and down in the air. Wagging its tail in quick, furious strokes, it scampered across the plaza to Elven, its black nose sniffing at her satchel. Thinking it must be hungry, Elven reached into her bag and held out the remains of her beef rib. The dog grabbed the bone with its mouth, ran around in a circle excitedly before standing on its hind legs to beg for more.

'That's a neat little trick!' Elven said with a sigh. 'But that's all I have.'

'He's a real clever one,' a woman's voice rang out across the plaza.

In the dim light, Elven saw a tall woman walking towards her. In one hand, she was holding onto the leashes of half a dozen dogs, all of them straining in different directions. Wound around her free forearm was a bundle of unused leashes.

'You must be new here.' The woman, who seemed to be in her late forties, looked her up and down with her piercing green eyes. Her hair was pulled back and tucked under her headscarf, exposing the handsome angles of her jaw and chin. A beauty spot marked the sharp precipice of her right cheekbone. There was an air of authority about her. If not for the coarse fabric of her dress, which looked wrinkled and worn thin by years of washing, Elven might have thought she was someone important.

'He's Gogo, and I'm Madam Green,' she said, holding out her hand.

'How do you do?' Elven, realizing that she had been staring, shook the woman's hand hurriedly. 'I'm Elven.'

'Elven . . . that's an interesting name.' The woman's face lit up with a smile. 'Does it derive from the word "elf"?'

'Actually, no.' Elven held up her left hand slowly, showing Madam Green her extra stump. 'The people at the orphanage named me that because I have eleven fingers,' she explained. Although she did not like talking about her deformity, there was something about Madam Green that made her feel both awed and at ease.

Madam Green nodded approvingly. 'It's a fitting name.'

Elven smiled, secretly relieved that Madam Green did not ask more. There were some people who wanted to know if she could wiggle her extra thumb (she couldn't), just so that they could make up clever jokes about how she would probably make a better pianist than them.

'I don't suppose this bench will make for a good night's sleep,' Madam Green said.

Elven felt her face turn a bright red. 'I don't have any money to pay the innkeeper,' she muttered. 'And I have no friends in this town.'

The awkward silence was punctuated by the dog's barking.

'Ah, Gogo begs to differ,' Madam Green said. 'He says you're his friend.'

'He does?'

Madam Green smiled and pointed to how Gogo was sniffing at Elven's shoes. 'See how much he likes you. And you gave him your food so you must think of him as a friend too.'

'What kind of dog is he?' Elven asked, running her fingers through Gogo's fur.

'He's half German Shepherd, and half something else,' the woman answered. 'Some people look down on mongrels but I say they make some of the bravest and most faithful companions I've ever known.'

Elven was about to reply when her stomach suddenly growled loudly. She looked away, embarrassed.

'Well, that settles it,' Madam Green chirped without missing a beat. 'Why don't you give me a hand, and we'll get you something to eat?' Before Elven could protest, Madam Green had pressed Gogo's leash into her palm.

'What do I do?' Elven asked, patting the dog on the head.

Gogo barked loudly and trotted over to Elven's satchel. Wagging his tail, he pushed the satchel towards her, as if asking her to hurry. Elven laughed and slung the bag over her shoulder.

'Where are we going?' she asked, looking up. But Madam Green and her dogs were already at the edge of the plaza. Elven half ran as she pushed her bicycle along, and Gogo followed in excitement.

They exited the plaza via a street next to the church, moving swiftly past houses that looked oddly lonely in the fading light of the day. The cobblestoned street soon gave way to a dirt road that grew steeper and decreasingly visible under the shin-high grass. When it got too dark, Madam Green lit a lantern with a match.

Before she knew it, Elven found herself deep in the mountain, walking between ancient trees so tall that they seemed to reach all the way to the stars. Except for the sounds of their feet crunching on fallen twigs and the occasional clicks of the bicycle chain, the forest was eerily quiet. Even the dogs were silent.

Pushing the bicycle uphill was beginning to make Elven's shoulders ache. With no destination in sight, the bare-bones comfort of the plaza bench suddenly seemed much more appealing. Why were they headed up the mountain? Did Madam Green live on the other side? It seemed unlikely that they were lost, but who was to say that Madam Green might not just park her on a stone slab with some dead leaves for cover?

'Don't worry,' Madam Green said without turning her head. 'Not far now.'

My goodness, Elven thought. *Is she a mind reader?*

Before long, a little house on stilts appeared in the distant clearing. Suddenly, the air was filled with maniacal howling and yelps. Up ahead, Madam Green was standing inside a fenced area surrounded by a moving swamp of shadows. Somehow, the half dozen dogs they brought back had multiplied into a colony of hounds. Elven shuddered and was about to break into a run when she felt Gogo push against her.

'What?' she asked Gogo. 'You think I'll lose my way in the dark?' He whined and remained resolutely still. 'I suppose I have no choice but to stay,' she muttered with resignation. 'But at least I'll have you by my side.'

Finally, after what seemed like eternity, Madam Green came out of the enclosure and shut the gate behind her.

'Sorry to keep you waiting,' she said. 'The dogs get so excited when I bring home new friends.'

'Are they all yours?' Elven asked, unable to contain her curiosity.

'They are, for now,' Madam Green said in an exhausted but happy voice.

'Is this a kennel?'

'I prefer the word "sanctuary".'

They went up a small dirt path, and up three steps to the front veranda of the house. Madam Green pulled open a glass door and then a timber one behind it. Just then, Gogo tore loose from Elven and made a beeline into the darkness of the house. *Woof, woof, woof,* he barked like a general commanding his troops.

'You impatient rascal,' Madam Green chided as she lit the kerosene lamps by the door. 'Why don't you show our guest around while I heat up dinner?'

It suddenly dawned on Elven that she had never been inside someone's home before. As Madam Green brought out the candles, she wandered around the house, drinking in all the furnishings and colours. The living room had worn timber flooring, and the walls were painted a robin-egg blue. Above, rough-hewn timber beams contrasted against the white of the ceiling. Two large rattan chairs with cushioned seats and a round table anchored the corner of the small living room.

Was a home supposed to be messy? Elven felt a compulsion to pick up the cushion that had fallen on the floor, but Gogo had already beaten her to it. With a flop, he sank into the worn velvet and let out a satisfied whimper.

An oil painting of a man and woman in elaborate costumes hung opposite the doorway. Elven wandered up to it, entranced by the vibrant green, blue, and yellow woven into their headgears.

'My great-grandparents,' Madam Green said, coming over. 'Have you seen the Cantorean costume before?'

'No,' said Elven, 'but it's beautiful.'

'Oh, yes.' Madam Green nodded. 'When the early Western settlers followed Abel Tanzania here in the seventeenth century, they brought with them their unique national dresses. There were the Mavarians in their dark blue and white wraps, the Ungalese with their billowing silk collars, and of course, the Cantoreans were the most striking with their tricoloured headscarves.'

'What about the Northerners?' Elven asked, thinking of Master Takuno.

'I'm not sure.' Madam Green removed her scarf to reveal a head of beautiful, wavy hair piled up in a bun. 'Most of them arrived only twenty years ago to work in the plantations.'

'I wish I could wear one of those ethnic dresses,' Elven said wistfully.

'Don't we all? I myself only wore one until I was eleven or twelve. Then, all of a sudden, it was no longer fashionable. A real pity, I say. Still, I'm glad the Natives continue to don their traditional costume on important days.'

'The Mawolis do?'

'Oh yes. During their celebrations on the summer and winter solstices, they decorate their bodies with the blue dye of the maliaki flower and dance in simple skirts fashioned from coconut husks.'

'They wear skirts made from fruits?' Elven said. 'Isn't that kind of primitive?'

'Well, cotton—from which you make cloth—is a vegetable,' Madam Green stated simply. 'When I was a young girl, my Mawoli nanny used to paint my arms with maliaki dye too.'

'Why would you let her do that?' Elven asked in shock.

'The maliaki flower symbolizes friendship in the Mawoli culture. Painting someone's body with its dye is an expression of your bond with them. In fact, I've got a maliaki bush growing near the kennel if you want to try it.'

Elven shook her head stiffly. 'No, thank you.' The last thing she wanted was to announce her background to the whole world.

'Well, silly me. I suppose children these days have better things to do.' Madam Green headed into the kitchen. 'But if you change your mind, let me know.'

Elven did not answer. What was Madam Green trying to hint at with all this talk about body painting?

She shook the thought from her head and hurried behind Madam Green.

In the kitchen was a wooden stove and oven, not unlike the one at the orphanage. Timber shelves lined the wall next to the door, filled with jars of spices and herbs. On the polished wooden counter, dried chilli, garlic, potatoes, and onions rested in rattan baskets next to a large fruit bowl. Pots and pans of all varieties and sizes hung from a cast iron rack bolted to the ceiling, giving the impression of a metallic forest. A mint green armoire stood next to the sink, and Elven was delighted to find a treasure trove of recipe books with faded, creased spines.

'May I take a look at these?' she asked, unable to contain her eagerness.

'Certainly.' The smell of meat and vegetables filled the air as Madam Green lifted the pot lid. 'Do you like cooking, my dear?'

'I love baking,' Elven said. She ran her fingers along the row of books, waiting for one to call out to her. 'I used to bake every day.'

'Ah, then, you will appreciate *Cookies and Kueh* by Bibik Lonoya.' Madam Green retrieved two dark green volumes from the shelf and showed them to Elven as they waited for the soup to heat up. 'These can be bedtime reading for you,' she chuckled.

Elven blinked, not quite trusting her ears. Did Madam Green just invite her to stay the night?

'You realize that I'm a runaway,' Elven confessed. If she was going to be thrown out, it might as well be sooner rather than later.

'I suppose it did occur to me fleetingly,' Madam Green said as she raised the soup ladle to her mouth. 'Hmm . . . perfect.'

'I don't want to get you into trouble . . .'

'You won't.' Madam Green placed the pot on the table and motioned for Elven to take a seat. Carefully, she scooped out two bowls of piping hot noodle soup.

'Don't just stand there!' she chided. 'The noodle soup's no good when it's cold.'

Elven sat down obediently, chastened by her host's hospitality.

'This is the most delicious thing I've ever eaten!' Elven exclaimed as she sipped the soup. 'I . . . I was just wondering . . .' she said, in between bites. 'Who do the dogs belong to?'

'People in town had them as pets,' Madam Green said. She fished out a piece of chicken from the pot and placed it in front of Gogo who was begging by the stove. 'Everyone loves puppies, don't they? But when those puppies grow into dogs and have minds of their own, they no longer seem so adorable. Some of the dogs chewed up their owners' furniture, others grew too loud, a few fell sick. Whatever the reason, their owners decided they no longer wanted them.'

Elven's mouth fell open. 'Just like that?'

'Oh, yes.' Madam Green wiped her hands on her apron and sat down opposite Elven. The wrinkles around her deep-set eyes suddenly seemed very pronounced under the flickering light. 'When owners no longer want their pets, they leave them in an open cage behind the Town Hall. At the end of the month, if nobody else adopts them, they're taken away . . .'

'Where to?'

Madam Green pursed her lips into a thin line and shook her head. 'You don't want to know.' She took out a piece of meat and fed it to Gogo.

Elven swallowed the rest of her soup, the injustice rubbing against her heart like a small stone in a shoe.

'Don't you fret. I try to get to them all, if I can. The ones here with me are safe.' Madam Green collected the empty bowls and gave Elven a smile. 'It's late, child. You'd better go to bed.'

With the lamp in her hand, Madam Green led Elven up the stairs. The old timber steps creaked and squeaked like nightingales under their weight.

In the attic, there was a small bed, a writing table, and a large chest tucked under the gently sloping roof. Madam Green knelt down in front of the chest and took out a nightgown embroidered with hibiscus flowers.

'How old are you?' she asked.

'Twelve.'

'This may be too small but try it anyway.' She left the room to give Elven some privacy.

Elven slipped out of her grubby clothes and into the nightgown. Looking into the tarnished mirror, she felt as if she had suddenly transformed into someone special—someone who had a future beyond scrubbing, mending, and cleaning.

There was a knock on the door and Madam Green stuck her head around.

'Yes, it's too short, isn't it?' She could not hide her disappointment at the sight of Elven's knobbly knees. 'Whatever was I thinking?'

'But it's roomy!' Elven cried. 'And the length is perfect for hot nights. It's such a beautiful nightgown.'

A faint smile flashed across Madam Green's face. 'Yes, it is.'

'Who does it belong to?' Elven twirled and the gown floated up around her, soft as petals. 'I hope its owner doesn't mind me wearing it.'

'No, she wouldn't . . . it was too big for her.' Madam Green's clear voice was suddenly hoarse. Looking embarrassed, she bade Elven good night and closed the door behind her.

Elven sat on the bed, listening to the fading footsteps. Under the flickering candlelight, the attic bedroom suddenly felt claustrophobic and prison-like. On the wall opposite the bed, she noticed a mural showing animals going up a mountain. At the top of the mountain, a little girl stood waiting, her head hidden by the clouds.

What a strange drawing, Elven thought as she huddled under the covers. *It's almost as if the girl's staring at me from behind the clouds.*

She blew out the candle and tried to block out the sea of questions churning in her mind. *Why is Madam Green so nice to me? Who does this nightgown belong to? Why isn't that girl here any more?*

A slant of moonbeam fell across the bed from the window, giving her the impression of being enveloped by a layer of soft white gauze.

As she was drifting off to sleep, Elven thought she heard some high-pitched voices and cackling in the distance. A shiver ran up her spine. If there really was a mountain witch, how would she protect herself? She scanned the room, looking for a makeshift weapon but found nothing suitable.

I have to stay awake. A few more hours and it'll be morning. Then, I'll be safe and headed to Bowler Hat Lake.

But soon, her eyelids grew heavy, and she was quickly overcome by a blanket of exhaustion. In the darkness, the voices never stopped calling out to her.

11

The Keeper of Birds

When Elven awoke, the sky was a canvas of violet and pink. Against this backdrop, the forest shimmered like a patina of soft, dewy green. Outside the window, a rooster crowed enthusiastically.

After a while, Elven made her bed, and with some reluctance, changed out of the nightgown and back into her dirty clothes. She headed down to the kitchen, where she saw Madam Green's thin frame bent over the chopping board. Sunlight poured in through the windows, illuminating the simple interiors. The salty aroma of animal fat filled the air.

'Good morning!' Madam Green greeted her with a smile. 'Did you sleep well?' She wiped her hands on her apron and, while humming, poured some tea out of an unglazed teapot.

'Very well, thank you.' Elven took the cup gratefully. The tea was strong and fragrant. It drew the lethargy out of her limbs and the sleep from her head.

She watched as her host fried up batches of mushrooms, beans, and toast in a cast-iron pan. When those were done, Madam Green took out a tray of crispy fried fish from the oven and divided it up between two plates.

'Fried fish?' Elven asked, surprised at Madam Green's generosity. The children in the orphanage were never allowed any fish. That was reserved strictly for the caretakers.

'You don't like it?' Madam Green asked.

'I like it,' Elven said quickly. 'I've not had any since I was five.' She blushed, for she had stolen that piece from the kitchen.

'Well, dig in, then.' Madam Green placed the overflowing plates on the table. 'You're not getting any younger!'

After breakfast, they took a walk outside, where Gogo and a few other dogs were busy chasing a ball. Madam Green pointed to the smallest dog—a black-and-white bull terrier.

'Look at Woody go!' Madam Green said with a proud smile. 'To think that he's almost blind.'

The garden was enclosed by a low, wooden fence. Leafy vegetables, carrots, and broccoli grew in long, neat rows, a contrast to the wild and natural lines of the forest. A small chicken coop lay at the far end of the garden, home to five hens, a rooster who could not stop preening in front of his new guest, and their brood of fluffy chicks.

'Would you like to see the parrots?' Madam Green asked.

'Parrots!' exclaimed Elven. 'Were they the voices I heard outside my window last night?'

Madam Green chuckled. 'Sometimes the wind carries their voices over to the house.'

Elven nodded sheepishly, remembering how she had worked herself up to a state of hysteria.

As they walked around the kennel to the back of the house, Elven asked, 'When you said that the dogs are yours "for now", what did you mean?'

'They don't stay with me forever, you see. In August, I bring them to meet new owners who'll take care of them.' Madam Green swung open the door of a cage the size of a large shed. 'The aviary, my lady,' she said with a curtsey.

Elven giggled and stepped inside. Two small and rather bare trees took up much of the space inside the cage. On their branches, several parrots paced about, gazing at their new visitor with questioning, intelligent eyes. A few of them walked up to Elven before huddling together in a corner, making furious clicking noises. It was as if they were having a meeting to decide whether she was friend or foe.

'Hello, Princess,' Madam Green said to an orange parakeet with a red head. 'You're a pretty bird, aren't you?'

'Pretty bird!' squawked Princess. 'Pretty pretty bird!'

Laughing, Elven ran forward to take a closer look. But she was startled to see that when Princess turned around, there was a bald patch on her chest that stretched almost all the way to her legs. Unlike the beautiful plumage that covered the rest of her body, her exposed chest was grey and bumpy.

'Who plucked off her feathers?' Elven asked, horrified.

'She did it herself,' Madam Green replied, her hand stroking Princess' back.

'What! But why?'

'Princess was heartbroken when her owners abandoned her,' Madam Green said in a low voice. 'For the first few months, I had to put her in a collar to stop her from plucking out more feathers.' Madam Green let Princess off on a branch and offered her some nuts from her apron pocket. 'Thankfully, she seems to have stopped mutilating herself.'

As Madam Green swept the aviary clean of the bird droppings, Elven took a closer look around the cage. It pained her to see that Princess was not the only one with missing plumage. A few birds still had their collars on—hard cardboard pieces that wrapped around their throats like funnels. Elven felt a lump in her throat. It was as if she were back at the orphanage, except this time, she was surrounded by parrots instead of children.

'Water!' a red parrot with yellow and blue wings squawked behind her. He grabbed a metal bowl with his beak and banged it against the tree trunk.

'Oh, you clever bird!' Elven cried, reaching out to stroke the parrot.

'No!' Madam Green shouted. The bird threw the bowl on the floor with a clatter and Elven jumped back. 'Tiger can be aggressive towards strangers. I'm sorry if he's frightened you. He feels protective of me, you see.'

'Does he bite?' Elven picked up the bowl while eyeing Tiger warily.

Madam Green gave a wry smile. 'Tiger certainly lives up to his name!' She took the bowl from Elven and filled it with water from a can. 'Truth is, they all do, at some point or another. Sadly, their owners don't understand that it's a phase. They grow angry and throw them out.' She set the bowl in the crook of the tree branch next to Tiger.

'Just like that!' Elven exclaimed, thinking very poorly of the Armorians. First, the dogs, then the birds. It seemed that affection often came with an end date in the Town of Love and Gold.

'How did Tiger end up here?'

'Well, we imported him from Mavaria. In fact, Tiger is the first scarlet macaw to ever step foot in Kalimasia. After we got ours, everyone in town wanted one. It became a status symbol of sorts. That is, until people realized how difficult it is to keep a wild bird.' Madam Green shook her head. 'We never should have started it.'

'Who's "we"?'

Madam Green's face fell and she stopped in her tracks. Elven bit her lips, wondering if she had said something wrong.

'Me and the man who used to own a store in Armora,' Madam Green said.

'The girl whom the nightgown belongs to . . . was she the one who wanted a pet parrot?' Elven asked.

'Yes,' Madam Green said, turning away to adjust a small mirror dangling on a branch. 'But she's not here to take care of Tiger any more.'

Instinctively, Elven knew she should change the topic. But the curious part of her just couldn't resist one last question.

'Where did she go?'

Madam Green stiffened. 'I don't know,' she said after a pause.

'I'm sorry,' Elven whispered. She didn't know what she was apologizing for but it felt like the right thing to do. 'You must miss—'

'Would you like to give me a hand with those branches?' Madam Green asked, spinning around. Her smile was painfully bright. 'We've got lots to do before lunch.'

Elven wanted to say something comforting to the older woman, but she thought better of it and got back to work. In silence, they cleared out the tree branches that had been plucked clean of fruit. It was tricky getting the branches through the narrow cage door, but somehow they managed with just minor scratches. Then, Madam Green led Elven to a new pile of fruit-bearing branches outside the shed, and together they hauled them back to the aviary.

'How do you manage to do everything by yourself?' Elven asked, exhausted.

Madam Green shrugged. 'It'll be easier once I find the dogs a new home at the Fossil Fair. You know, that annual event at Bowler Hat Lake—'

'Bowler Hat Lake!' cried Elven. 'Why, that's where Master Takuno is. That's where I need to go today!'

'Do you, love? And why is that?' Madam Green was looking at her with a gentle expression.

'Well, you see I have a—' Elven paused, wondering if she ought to reveal her secret. She gazed up at the kind face before her and knew at once that she had no reason not to. 'I have a Puzzle Box that can't be opened.'

She took the box out of her pocket and, sensing Madam Green's perplexity, launched into a detailed explanation about its mechanism. When she finished, Madam Green looked as if she was trying to recall something. 'I saw a stall at the Fossil Fair last year selling handmade boxes. Though I cannot say for sure if it was Takuno's stall or not.'

'It must have been his! There's no one else who can make them like him!' Elven paced up and down the aviary, wringing her hands. 'Oh, I must get to the fair. That way, I can get him to open mine. He must remember the correct Key, he must!'

'And you say this Key is the reason why your mother loves you?'

'Yes, it's a tradition of sorts. The Key is a word that explains why the giver loves the receiver. But I never knew her. And so, I don't know the reason.'

'But why does she need a reason?' Madam Green asked, shaking her head. 'She's your mother.'

Elven stopped in her tracks.

'Maybe my mother had no reason,' she muttered. 'Maybe that's why it won't open.'

'I'm sorry, child. I wish I could help you.' Madam Green looked thoughtful for a moment, and perhaps a little sad. 'Well, I really shouldn't be holding you back from your adventure. If you want to cross the mountain before sundown then you should set off right away. I will pack you enough food and water to last you till the lake.'

She paused and gave Elven's shoulder a squeeze. 'Thank you for helping out with the birds.'

'It was fun . . .' Elven replied softly. Until now, she had no idea that any work outside the kitchen could be so enjoyable.

'Then, I will see you in three weeks?' Madam Green added hopefully. 'I will be at the fair with the dogs. I know Gogo will be glad to see you again.'

'But how are you going to walk there with so many dogs?' Elven asked, surprised.

Madam Green laughed. 'See that little fellow there?' She pointed to a grey pigeon in a smaller cage outside the aviary. 'That's Kraw. He belongs to my friend in the capital. When I'm ready to leave, I'll send him off with a message so my friend will know when to pick me up in his wagon. It'll be impossible to carry all my baked goods there without his help.'

'What will you be baking?' Elven asked, suddenly missing the sticky feel of dough on her fingers.

'Oh, cakes and muffins. The fairgoers love variety, you see. If I can get them to buy more, I'll be able to earn a tidy sum—enough to rescue more dogs.'

Elven looked out of the aviary. Her heart suddenly felt heavy, as if it were anchored to the ground beneath her. In the distance came the barking of dogs eager for food and exercise. Three weeks felt like a long time, but it was not forever.

'Perhaps the fairgoers might fancy my rainbow cake,' she said. 'And perhaps we could journey together to Bowler Hat Lake?'

12

The Road to the Lake

For the next three weeks, Elven stayed with Madam Green on Mount Armora. She learned to climb trees and cut down fruit-bearing branches for the parrots. When the weather was good and the sun inviting, Elven and Madam Green would walk down to the creek with Gogo and have lunch there. Gogo loved splashing in the cool water and would always try to get them in too. Madam Green was not much of a swimmer and often complained that she was too old to be frolicking among fishes. But Elven relished the dog's attention and would indulge Gogo even on days when the water was far too chilly.

She also grew to be a good fisherwoman. With a spear in hand, Elven became quite adept at catching the schools of trout that populated the water. One time, she even caught a couple of eels, which Madam Green broiled and served with sweet potatoes. The snake-like creatures were surprisingly succulent!

There was much to be done to get the farm in order, but amid the washing, mending, and cleaning, Madam

Green found time to surprise Elven with floral dresses sewn from flour sack fabrics. It was such a novelty to be dressed in anything other than a uniform that Elven could not help preening in front of the mirror every time she walked past it.

With Madam Green's guidance and companionship, time flew by uneventfully. Only one unusual incident stood out during Elven's stay on Mount Armora.

It was a typical day and the evening had ended with Elven working on the Puzzle Box in bed after a hot bath. As she broke up and reassembled the tiles in different sequences to form YOU ARE MINE again and again, Elven grew increasingly frustrated. Despite her best efforts, the box had refused to open yet again. After the fourth attempt, she tossed it into her satchel and closed her eyes.

But sleep would not come to her. Finally, she sat up, hungry. Hoping to find some leftovers from dinner, Elven crept back down the staircase, stopping only when she heard a strange sound in the dark. Startled, she crouched down and peered around the wall.

A soft light from the lamp illuminated the kitchen. At the dining table, Madam Green sat hunched over a small, red box, her face buried in her palms. If not for the violent trembling of her shoulders, Elven would not have guessed that she was crying. Even in her grief, Madam Green was restrained.

Elven felt an urge to put her arms around the older woman but she knew that her presence would only make things awkward. In the end, she crept back into bed, hating herself for her cowardice.

* * *

Before long, the three weeks had flown by, and it was time to head to Bowler Hat Lake. On the morning they were due to set off, a large man named Mr Bora arrived at the house in a wagon drawn by two fine-looking horses.

'Ah, you've got yourself a companion, Madam Green!' Mr Bora boomed, jumping off his wagon. 'And here's mine, coming back to you.' He reached into the wagon bed and brought out a small cage holding Kraw the pigeon. Despite his leonine mane of white hair, Mr Bora was bristling with the energy of a young man.

'This is Elven,' Madam Green said, taking over the cage. 'She'll be joining us on our trip.'

'Excellent!' Mr Bora bent down, extended his large hand and gave hers a few pumps. 'Let me guess, you're a fossil hunter?'

'A fossil hunter?' Elven asked, glancing at Madam Green for help.

'Madam Green!' Mr Bora exclaimed in mock disbelief. 'Have you not explained the Fair's glorious history to our young friend?'

'Not really. And you mustn't give her the impression that we're visiting an archaeology site.' A faint smile floated across Madam Green's lips. 'Or that we'll even see any dinosaurs. Triceratops or Carrot-tops or whatever you call them.'

'Every piece of history needs to be told.' Mr Bora stuck his hand into a cracked leather satchel hanging off the wagon and, after digging around, produced a crumpled roll of newspaper.

'Bowler Hat Lake is said to be the oldest crater lake in the country,' Mr Bora read in a solemn voice, 'formed by a fiery meteorite crashing into the earth as dinosaurs roamed the planet. Two hundred million years later, mankind replaced the mighty creatures as the main visitors to the lake. Archaeologists and amateur fossil hunters would traverse the shores of Bowler Hat Lake, digging out bones of extinct plants and creatures trapped and preserved in the lakeside rocks. So famous was Bowler Hat Lake for its scientific discoveries that every year, in the last week of summer, scientists and wealthy merchants from all corners of the world would make the much anticipated journey there in order to trade precious fossils.'

He stuffed the papers back into the satchel with a smile. 'Now,' Mr Bora said, turning to Madam Green, 'let's get started, shall we?'

With swift, sturdy hands, Mr Bora loaded up the crates of baked goods while Madam Green placed Kraw back into his home. Then, Mr Bora carefully covered the crates with a tarpaulin before they allowed the dogs into the wagon. At last, they were on their way, with Elven seated snugly between the adults.

'You know, Elven,' Madam Green said hesitantly. 'I don't want you to think that you're going to an old-fashioned county fair filled with artisans and craftsmen plying their wares. Ever since the completion of the railroad tracks, the Fossil Fair has ballooned into this gargantuan event with cheap food, factory-produced merchandise, and money-sucking arcades.'

Mr Bora nudged Elven playfully with his left elbow. 'Don't you listen to her, dear. I get plenty of exotic spices and produce from the Fossil Fair, well enough to uphold my restaurant's reputation.'

Elven's eyes widened. 'Are you a cook, Mr Bora?'

'He's a famous chef,' Madam Green said with a smile. 'He owns Fhakawaiwai in Kenden.'

Elven laughed. 'Fhakawaiwai? What a delightful name! What does it mean?'

Mr Bora steered the horses around a fallen tree and turned to Elven with a wink. 'It means "mouth-watering" and "delicious" in Mawoli.'

Elven frowned. 'Mawoli? But why Mawoli?'

'Because I'm one-quarter Mawoli.'

Elven could not help but stare at Mr Bora's profile. He had a sharp, refined nose, high cheekbones, and a pinkish complexion that was more Cantorean than Native. 'But you don't even look it!'

'A great loss,' Mr Bora said.

The genuine regret in Mr Bora's voice surprised Elven. Why would anyone want to tell the whole world he was a quarter-Mawoli? Wouldn't that be bad for business? Perhaps Madam Green was exaggerating. Surely someone with Mr Bora's background could not be *that* famous.

'My grandmother was Mawoli,' Mr Bora continued, mistaking Elven's confusion for admiration. 'It was she who taught me how to cook. Some of the most popular recipes in my restaurant come from her.'

'Even the governor has dined at Fhakawaiwai,' Madam Green added.

Were they pulling her leg? Why would such a high-ranking official dine in a Mawoli restaurant of all places?

'Then, he can't possibly know that you are a half-breed,' she said.

'Elven!' Madam Green exclaimed. 'That's a racist term!'

Elven's face burned in embarrassment. 'But everyone uses it.'

'Doesn't mean it's right,' Madam Green replied gently.

'It's not her fault,' Mr Bora said in a sympathetic voice, which made Elven want to shrivel up and disappear. 'It's all she's been taught in the orphanage.' He paused and looked meaningfully at Elven. 'Everyone, including the governor, knows I'm half Cantorean, one-quarter Ungalese, and one-quarter Mawoli.'

So three-quarters Western, Elven thought darkly. Oh, what she would give to look more Westerner and less Native!

'What about you, Elven?' Mr Bora asked. 'What's your heritage?'

'Mavarian.'

The horses slowed to a trot as they rounded a precipitous cliff face.

'I know you are shocked,' Mr Bora said into the silence. 'You are wondering how someone like me can be so successful.'

'I didn't say that,' Elven protested weakly.

Mr Bora turned and smiled at her. 'I'm not angry at you, Elven. I used to be angry when people questioned my ancestry but not any more. I've decided to not let society tell me what I can or cannot do.'

'But you can't be anything if people have boxed you as one thing,' Elven retorted. *Like when I tried to get a job at the bakery and got mistaken for a thief.* 'What can you do if people don't even give you a chance because of the way you look?'

'Then, you've got to make your own chance, dear,' Mr Bora replied slowly.

'Mr Bora started out as a street vendor,' Madam Green added.

'And before that I was a bum, a good-for-nothing who got into fights defending my so-called "tribal pride". But thank goodness, my late-grandmother managed to knock some sense into me. "You've got nothing to be ashamed of," she scolded me, "and I'm tired of you ranting at the Westerners for taking our land. Stop blaming other people, lad."'

'The Westerners stole land from the Mawolis?' Elven asked, horrified. 'But this wasn't in our textbooks . . .'

'Aye, few things are in the textbooks. They stole land and a whole lot more.' Mr Bora shook his head fiercely, as if to rid himself of the unpleasant thoughts. 'But things are changing in Kalimasia. That's what the governor said to me when I served him my grandmother's grilled fish. And I'm not agreeing with him simply because he ate my food. It's true. I've seen it in the capital. In the faces of my patrons and in the faces of their children. If we unshackle ourselves from the past, we'll all have a brighter future. Do you know what I mean?'

Elven nodded, more because she didn't want to prolong the argument. She couldn't let go of the past—not until she solved the Puzzle Box. And to do that, she had to keep her Mawoli blood hidden as best as she could. She thought of the warm welcome Mr Long had given her at the Heritage Museum. Would he have treated her that way if he didn't think she was Mavarian? And what about Master Takuno? Would a respected person like him help someone like her? No, there was too much at stake.

Still, Mr Bora's conviction had given her a glimmer of hope. Maybe one day in the far future, she would be able to tell people that she was half Mawoli. For now, she would just have to hold on to Mr Bora's assurances and guard her secret like a flickering flame.

Just then, the wagon exited a grove of ancient pines and burst out onto a flat, open field dotted with orange wildflowers. After weeks of being up in the mountain, the sun felt warm and glorious. Even the tumultuous thoughts seemed to evaporate under the heat. Elven sighed in pleasure.

'Gee up, horsies!' boomed Mr Bora, driving the horses across the field. 'Gee up!'

'At your own pace, Mr Bora.' Madam Green stretched her hands up high, as if trying to touch the clouds above them. 'We're very grateful for this annual ride. Very grateful indeed.'

'Glad to be of service. I'll get you ladies there before noon!'

If I survive this ride, thought Elven as she hung on to the edge of her seat.

'Do you know what truffles are, Elven?' Madam Green asked as they drove past a small hill with charred and blackened tree trunks.

'Pieces of bunched up cloth?'

'That's ruffles. Truffles are a kind of very rare and expensive mushroom. One of Mr Bora's most well-known dishes is his truffle chestnut soup.'

'Ah, yes, I modified it from a traditional Mawoli recipe. If I had my way, I'd use black morels.' A wistful smile appeared across Mr Bora's face. 'Do you remember that bumper crop I found after that summer fire?'

'Of course I do. You made quite a first impression with that huge wicker basket on your back.' Turning to Elven, Madam Green added, 'Forest fires are great for morel mushrooms; not so great for mountain folks like me.'

'I have a friend who loves gathering wild mushrooms,' Elven said, thinking of Coal. 'We don't have truffles or morels back in the orphanage, but Coal is really inventive. He makes the most delicious stock from wild thyme and mushrooms. And he bakes the portabellas with ground meat and garlic. They're so delicious!'

She wished Coal could visit Mount Armora. He would love its cornucopia of wild mushrooms and edible plants. She added up the days until his birthday and was heartened to know she wouldn't have to wait long. In a month's time, he would turn sixteen and make his way to Armora.

'Perhaps he might like to apprentice with me one day,' Mr Bora suggested. 'I'm always on the lookout for talented and hard-working assistants.'

'Oh, that would be wonderful!' cried Elven. If Coal became an apprentice chef at the famous Fhakawaiwai, his future would be secured. 'I can just imagine him swooning over those truffles!'

'Just wait till you catch a whiff of those black diamonds,' Mr Bora said. 'They're like a heady mix of dark chocolate, wine, and aged cheese.'

'If only we could smell them without being crushed by a thousand sweaty bodies,' Madam Green groaned. She opened her travelling tin and offered some cookies to them.

'Ah, but it is precisely the "thousand sweaty bodies" who will adopt your dogs and buy your cakes!' Mr Bora steadied the horses with his right hand while grabbing a cookie with his left. 'Do you know what those fossil enthusiasts have in common with your dogs?'

'What?' asked Elven.

'They are only interested in bones!' Mr Bora said.

The three of them laughed and the dogs yelped enthusiastically from the wagon, eager to join in. Elven leaned behind and threw them pieces of cookies.

'Don't worry,' she leaned over and whispered to the Labrador closest to her. 'Soon, you'll have a new home and all the treats you'd ever want. And you don't even have to open a Puzzle Box.'

13

Abe and the Revelation

They rode along at breakneck pace for the next hour, overtaking groups of travellers in assorted buggies and carts. Finally, Elven spotted a flash of water beyond the roadside trees. As she craned her neck to get a better view, the wagon rounded a bend.

'Look!' exclaimed Madam Green.

Elven turned and let out a cheer. There, shimmering in the distance, was Bowler Hat Lake in its full glory. True to its name, the crater lake sat deep in a perfectly round depression in the landscape, bringing to mind a hat filled with liquid.

'In the past, that cliff face rising from the water would be crawling with fossil hunters suspended from ropes and pulleys,' Mr Bora said. 'It was quite a sight.'

Even from the road, Elven could see that the fairground above the lake was tightly packed with tents. Some were as large as mansions while others were as compact as sheds. When the wind blew, they rippled like waves of white and pink. In the middle, a Ferris wheel turned slowly, as if it were a water mill powered by this fabric ocean.

Elven reached inside her cloth bag and ran her fingers across the veneer of the Puzzle Box. Was Master Takuno there, somewhere in that coloured sea?

Approaching the gates of the fairground, they were greeted by the strains of live music. Madam Green handed a letter to the man at the entrance, who waved them through. They drove on a path of flattened grass, past stalls selling corn on the cobs, rainbow-coloured confections, fried bananas, and racks of grilled meat. Elven had never seen such ostentatious display of abundance. She sighed and swallowed a glob of saliva.

'Ah, there's Mr Ochre,' Madam Green said, pointing to an old man seated behind a table under a tent. Framing the perimeter of the tent was a low fence put together with rocks and recycled wood. The sign next to him read 'Dogs for Adoption'.

'Why do people of Cantorean descent have colour-related last names like Azure, Sienna, and Cerulean?' Elven asked.

'I'm not sure. But it probably has something to do with our headgear's colours.' With that, Madam Green hopped off the wagon and gave the old man a kiss on his cheek. 'Such a lovely tavern for the dogs! What would we do without friends like you?'

'No trouble at all,' he replied. 'I see you've got a good number of them dogs this year.'

'Yes, unfortunately.' Madam Green took out a loaf of bread from one of the crates. 'Well this is for your trouble, helping me set up year after year. Even if it was no trouble at all.' There was a moment of bantering and shuffling as the old man tried to reject her gift. But, in the end, he was won over by Madam Green's persistence. With a smile, he left with the loaf tucked under his arm.

Elven and Madam Green herded the dogs into the enclosure. Gogo, smart dog that he was, refused to go with the others, and so they let him scamper around as they laid out their baked goods on the table. Mr Bora, in the meantime, had gone off in search of his truffles.

Minutes passed, then half an hour. A few children stared curiously at the dogs but ran away when Elven tried to talk to them. The adults, on the other hand, only had eyes for the baked goods. Elven's rainbow cake sold out within the hour, so did most of the pastries. Few people were interested in the dogs. The ones who were seemed to find them too thin or too fat, too dull or too spotted.

'I'm not sure anyone will take them,' Elven grumbled.

'Faith, my child, faith,' Madam Green placed a hand on Elven's shoulder. 'If they come, they come. If they don't then we're none the poorer.'

Elven made a face, then climbed onto the chair so that she could have a better view of the fairgrounds. 'But how much longer do we have to wait here? How am I going to find Master Takuno if nobody comes for the dogs?'

'So that's why you're still waiting around here!' Madam Green said. 'Don't let us keep you, love. You must look for your Puzzle Box maker before it gets dark. I believe I saw his stall in the Northern Pavilion.' She dug out some money from her purse and pressed it into Elven's hand. 'Here, buy yourself something to eat too.'

Elven gave Madam Green a hug. 'But won't you be hungry?'

'Stop worrying and go!' Madam Green said, giving Elven a playful push.

Elven jogged past the amusement park, coins jiggling in her pocket. As she watched the fairgoers try their luck at one game or another, her stomach made a series of low growls. She decided to make her way towards the food stalls, guided by the mouth-watering aroma of hot meat and warm bread. For a long while, she stood frozen with indecision. She had never before seen such a large variety of food in one place, much of which had exotic, unpronounceable names. She moved from stall to stall, nibbling from tasting plates until she was satiated.

'Free drinks at the Northern Pavilion!' A promoter pressed a flyer into Elven's hand. 'Fuchsia tent to your right.'

'Northern Pavilion?' Elven repeated, her heart skipping a beat.

'Yes, that big fuchsia tent there,' the promoter said with a vague nod towards the cliff.

'Uh, okay. Pink tent to my right?'

'Fuchsia.' The promoter pointed to the cluster of large tents next to the roller coaster. 'Not rose, not salmon. Fuchsia.'

'What's the difference?' Elven called out. But the promoter had disappeared into the crowd.

Clutching the flyer, Elven made her way under the roller coaster tracks to the entrance of the Northern Pavilion.

'Greetings, visitor!' A woman in a long, elegant robe greeted her with a deferential bow next to the entrance. 'Welcome to the Northern Pavilion!' she said, her pinched cherry mouth widening into a smile across her face, which had been painted white.

As Elven walked into the tent, she wondered if the woman was some sort of clown, only prettier. Apparently, she was not the only one in costume. Here and there, young women in shimmering robes flitted around selling food and beverages. Above them, rice paper lanterns cast an orange glow over the straw canopies of the stalls. On a low stage, a musician was strumming pensively on a short-necked lute. Behind him was a long painting of the Northern continent populated with villagers and warriors. There were a few chairs scattered around but most of the visitors had abandoned their shoes on the grass and were seated cross-legged on the straw mats.

Elven wandered up and down the rows of stalls selling everything from horsehair calligraphy brushes to silk scarves. Finally, she spotted a vendor whose table was piled high with wooden ornaments like keychains and flutes. In the middle of these rather common objects was a large display box. And in that box was a collection of puzzle boxes not unlike hers!

'Excuse me,' she called out to the youth manning the stall. 'Do you speak English?'

'Why? Do *you*?' the lad replied in a perfect Kalimasia accent.

Elven blushed. 'I . . . I just assumed—'

'Yes, yes, assume away,' he muttered, rolling his eyes. 'And while you're at it, why not assume it's the Westerners who labour away at your vineyards?'

Elven took a deep breath. 'Are these real puzzle boxes?' she asked, ignoring what sounded like a snipe.

The lad did not answer but instead hollered in the direction of the opposite stall. 'ABE! CUSTOMER! She speaks ENGLISH!'

A short man with spiky hair popped his head out between a display of straw hats. 'Eh?' He lumbered over, rubbing his palms with a solicitous smile as the youth slipped away, sulking. 'Sorry about him. Growing pains,' he apologized. 'Looking to customize a puzzle box?'

'No, no. I'm looking for Master Takuno. Are these his works?'

Abe's face grew solemn. 'Yes, they are. But the Master is no longer with us.'

Elven blinked in disbelief. 'He moved again? Where?'

'My uncle . . . Master Takuno passed away yesterday,' Abe said quietly. 'A heart attack.'

14

A Riddle Disguised

'Yesterday?' Elven repeated in shock. 'But I came all the way here for his help!'

She fought to hold back her tears, but they broke loose and fell on the polished veneer of a timber bowl. 'I'm sorry,' she said, wiping them away with her fingers.

Abe seemed to be dumbstruck by her outburst. But as her sobs subsided, he said gently, 'It's been a shock to us too.' He handed her a grubby handkerchief from his pocket. Elven shook her head and wiped her face against the back of her hand. 'You can still buy them, you know,' Abe added helpfully.

'It's not that . . . I just wanted to ask him about . . .' Elven took out the Puzzle Box from her satchel and handed it to Abe. 'Can you solve this?'

Abe's mouth fell open. He turned the Puzzle Box around in this palm, shaking his head and clicking his tongue in admiration. 'This is one of his smallest. He must have made it a long time ago, when his eyesight was much better. Look at the craftsmanship . . . the sheer mastery of technique.'

He pushed the wooden tiles around expertly. 'Uncle must have been very happy when he made it.' He smiled, as if recalling a distant memory. 'He used to say, "When the spirit is simple with joy, the hands will master the complexity." The five-by-three Key is one of the most complicated to craft.'

Elven's stomach tightened into a dead knot. The hope that she had held onto so naively was fast disappearing, as if caught in a quicksand. 'So, can you open it?' she asked, her voice barely a whisper.

'I'm sorry, I can't.' Abe took a last appreciative look before handing the box back. 'You need to know the Key.'

'But the Key is here! YOU ARE MINE. I must have tried rearranging it a hundred times.'

'And it doesn't open?' Abe asked in a gentle voice.

'No.'

'Ah.' A smile spread slowly across Abe's wide face. 'Then, it must be an anagram. My uncle sometimes used them on special commissions.'

'Meaning?'

'Meaning it's a riddle disguised as a solution.'

'So this has nothing to do with placing the tiles in the right sequence?'

'The five-by-three is already complicated enough,' Abe said, his eyes wide. 'To make it a sequence box is to turn it into a torture instrument!'

Elven nodded with a grimace. The last three weeks had indeed been a torment for her.

'Now,' Abe continued, taking the box from Elven, 'if you're able to shift the tiles around until they form other words . . .' He began to push the tiles around, his brows furrowed in concentration.

'Look!' he cried, turning the top of the box towards Elven. 'I RENAME YOU!'

'That's the Key?' Elven asked, bewildered. *My mother loves me because she changed my name?*

'That's just an example.'

Elven sighed.

'Well, I'll let you in on a secret.' Abe leaned forward, his eyes twinkling. 'Sometimes, those words could be a *name*.'

'A name? What name?'

'Any name. Which is why I can't help you crack it. But what I can tell you is that my uncle did create Keys that were people's names. I'm not saying yours is like that, but if it is, and if you get it right, the whole box will spring open by itself.' Abe splayed open his fingers with a grin. 'Like a flower.'

Elven stared at the box, a lump rising in her throat. 'There are thousands, maybe millions of names in the world . . .'

'You're not trying out millions of names,' Abe comforted her. 'Only those that have ten letters.'

What words or names could she make from a ten-letter anagram? This was going to be much harder than she thought.

* * *

When she returned to the tent, Elven found Madam Green and Mr Bora deep in conversation next to the empty enclosure.

'You've always put the welfare of others above your own,' she heard him say as she approached from behind. 'First the animals and now the orphan.'

Elven froze. Madam Green said something in a low voice and Mr Bora was about to reply when she spotted Elven.

'Ah, there you are!' Madam Green called out.

Mr Bora turned, looking slightly flustered.

He's wondering how much I've overheard, Elven thought as she greeted them.

'Did you find Master Takuno?' Madam Green asked.

'He passed away yesterday.'

Madam Green's eyes widened in surprise. 'What happened?'

'It doesn't matter.' Elven slumped onto the grass, suddenly exhausted. She didn't want to tell them about the anagram, at least not until she had time to re-examine the box. 'Where are the dogs?' she asked, changing the subject.

'Woody and Gogo are sleeping next to the wagon.' Madam Green said. 'The rest have found new homes.'

'They're gone? All of them?'

Madam Green looked taken aback by Elven's reaction. 'Oh, I'm so sorry, my dear. I didn't think you'd want to say goodbye to them.'

'I didn't expect . . .'

'I'm sorry, I should have waited,' Madam Green said rather helplessly.

Elven knew she ought to be happy for the dogs, but the shock of losing her friends made her feel as if her half-empty heart had been completely hollowed out.

'Doggie! Look at that doggie!'

A boy sporting a pair of milk-bottle glasses was sprinting across the grass towards them. Behind him, a well-dressed elderly couple was struggling to keep up. In one swift motion, the boy produced a biscuit from his pocket and thrust it under Gogo's nose.

'Careful, Tao!' the old man shouted, almost tripping over his feet.

Gogo gulped down the biscuit and wagged his tail in approval. The old couple let out a collective sigh, visibly relieved that he wasn't going to tear their grandson to bits.

'Can we bring him home?' the boy asked.

'No!' Elven scrambled to her feet and ran towards them. Not Gogo! She had already lost Takuno today. She couldn't afford to lose her best friend. 'He's mine.' Elven swooped in and wrapped her arms around Gogo.

'But someone told us that these dogs are up for adoption!' the boy retorted. He turned to his grandfather with a pleading look, his face suddenly red.

'Have you already adopted this dog?' the old man asked in a kindly voice.

'No, but—' Elven found herself stuttering. Gogo belonged to Madam Green. If Madam Green wanted to give him away, she had no right to object. But why would Madam Green give Gogo away? He had always slept in the house, away from the other dogs. Elven had assumed that this made him special, that this same privilege extended to him not being given away. But those were simply assumptions. *Her* assumptions. And, so far, all her assumptions had been wrong.

She glanced at the boy, then at Madam Green who had made her way over. She was stupid to not have discussed this with Madam Green before they left Mount Armora. So stupid.

'But, darling, don't you think he's a little loud?' the grandmother said with a tight-lipped smile.

'Oh, he has the loudest bark,' Elven cried. She ignored Madam Green's raised eyebrows and rambled on, 'On some nights, you can't even get him to stop. And he eats everything.'

'I must say he is quite a bundle of energy,' the grandfather said. 'We used to have a bull terrier and she was the gentlest creature. She was Tao's best friend until she passed away last year.'

At the mention of his dog, Tao's mouth started quivering. 'I want Peppers back,' he whined, tears welling up behind his glasses. 'If I can't have Peppers back then I want this dog.' He ran forward and tried to grab Gogo's collar.

'He's not up for adoption!' Elven cried, pushing him away. Tao fell back with a thud and started wailing. 'I'm so sorry . . .' She tried to help him up but the angry boy would not have her near him. Just then, a black-and-white creature appeared from under the wagon, its sleepy eyes widening at the mayhem. It saw the crying boy, scampered over on its short legs and started licking his face. Startled, Tao began to giggle.

'Can I have him?' Tao asked, stroking Woody's fur. He stole a nervous glance at Elven who, despite feeling sorry, managed to rearrange her features into a scowl.

'Why, yes, he's up for adoption,' Madam Green said, ignoring the exchange. 'But I must tell you a few things about him first. Woody's blind in one eye—'

'My eyes aren't great either,' Tao replied to his grandparents' amusement.

Squatting down next to Elven, the elderly man said, 'I hope you're all right with us taking Woody home.'

Elven nodded. 'You be a good boy, Woody,' she said, giving the bull terrier a goodbye hug. 'I'll miss you.'

She fastened his collar with a leash and handed him to Tao. Sitting next to Gogo, she watched the trio walk Woody away with a heavy heart. If only her problems could be resolved so easily. Nothing was panning out for her. The only person who knew how to open her Puzzle Box was dead and going back to the orphanage was no longer an option. What was she to do now?

15

The Unexpected Visitors

At Madam Green's insistence, Elven returned to Mount Armora and continued helping out with the chores. With the dogs gone, she had the afternoons free to tinker with her Puzzle Box. But no matter how hard she tried, OUR MAIN EYE and I RUE A MONEY were just about the most sensible phrases she could produce. As for names, she could not think of any that were longer than NORA.

One day, as she was out cutting fruits for the parrots, Elven heard an unfamiliar rumble cutting through the humid stillness of the forest. Whether it was a well-honed instinct for avoiding trouble or an unwillingness to engage with the townsfolk, something told Elven she had to get off the mountain trail. She gathered up her baskets and ran behind a large bush. A minute later, a wagon appeared, two mules at the front kicking up a cloud of dirt as they moved sure-footedly up the mountain. A large, middle-aged man sat up front holding the reins, a cigarette dangling from the corner of his mouth. Riding behind him were three other men in wide-brimmed hats. The driver brought his whip down on the mules that whinnied and cantered past Elven, narrowly missing a squirrel out gathering nuts.

Elven did not move. She knew that a large tree, which had fallen during last week's thunderstorm, would make the road impassable. It was only a matter of minutes before the wagon would have to turn around. And a good thing, too, for she did not like the idea of those men getting too close to the cottage.

Sure enough, frustrated shouts rang out uphill as the driver urged the mules around. However, instead of heading back down the mountain, the wagon pulled up to a spot near her. The driver hopped out and christened the forest floor with a globule of phlegm. His face was as tough as a piece of overcooked hog jerky.

'You sure this is a good place?' he asked, turning to his companions.

'It's about as near as you can get to the creek,' answered the shortest man among them. His face was half covered in shadow because of his hat. Only his full, fleshy lips that looked almost rubbery were visible.

The other men paced around the site, glancing at the forest surrounding them, but remained non-committal.

'Fine. We dig them ditches there.' The driver pointed up the slope. 'Just before the creek winds towards the road.'

'I don't know, Skunk,' one of them said as he removed his hat to show a bald head and shifty eyes. 'Seems like a lot of trouble for something nobody's sure of.'

'Haven't they already found all the gold there is to find thirty years ago?' asked another. He was tall, with a limp ponytail that was more eel-like than a fairy-tale princess'.

The man named Skunk snorted. 'You see that patch there?' He pointed at the steep drop where a large piece of bare land stood out like a desert among the greenery. 'That's the old pit where the big guys were digging before the protests drove them out.'

'You're certain there is gold?' asked the bald man.

'As certain as my ma's a woman,' Skunk said with a scowl. 'The treasure ain't uncovered yet. All we need to do is enlarge the area. Clear those trees over there, give the mountain face a wash with the water cannon, and the gold will come tumbling out. This is your crack at being rich, lads. Either you're in or you're out. So, what do you say?'

One by one, the men nodded.

'Good,' said Skunk, his scowl disappearing. 'Once we bring up the pipes tomorrow, we can divert the water to a ditch there'—Skunk gestured towards the creek bend—'and channel it down to the pit.'

The men gave him a blank stare.

'Like a waterfall?' the bald man asked.

'How can this be better than the cradle?' the short man with the rubbery lips added.

Skunk snorted derisively. 'Fellas, you need to catch up with the times. Forget about the cradle! The water cannon is the only way to get rich quick.'

The bald man shook his head. 'I still don't understand—'

'How many times do I have to explain this?' Skunk cut in. 'Look, the water goes into a three-foot pipe as it flows downhill, then a two-foot pipe, then a one-footer. As the pipe diameter narrows, the water picks up speed. By the time it rushes through my cannon's five-inch nozzle, the water could easily pack a punch of five thousand pounds against the mountain face. That's enough pressure to wreck a house.'

'Blimey,' said the short man. 'Just how much water are we channelling?'

''Bout sixteen thousand gallons a minute.'

The bald man whistled appreciatively.

'That's like two railroad tank cars,' the man with the ponytail chipped in.

Skunk clapped him on the back, looking pleased. 'Now, since we're here, Moldylocks, we might as well build half the sluice.'

'Why not the entire sluice?' Moldylocks replied, flicking his ponytail. 'That'll allow us to get a head start before the Moles arrive.'

'You're an ambitious one.' Skunk gave a loud wheezing laugh and the men followed suit. 'Well, ambition is what we need. We'll finish the sluice today and widen the pit tomorrow.'

Elven frowned, unsure of what she had just overheard. But the men reminded her of a pack of hyenas, and she was glad she had stayed hidden.

'With luck, we'll have all the gold out of this mountain by winter.' Skunk hopped on the wagon and gave an impatient wave. 'Downhill, lads! Let's get really close to *our* gold pit.'

'Out with the gold!' hooted Moldylocks, pumping his fist in the air.

Talking excitedly about what they would buy when they were all rich, the men piled back into the wagon, which tore down the mountain trail jiggling this way and that.

* * *

A bad feeling seized Elven. She flew back to the house where she found Madam Green weeding in the garden.

'Why, Elven, your face's all red,' Madam Green said, looking up in surprise, 'Whatever's the matter?'

'A sluice!' Elven cried. 'They're . . . building a sluice—whatever that is!'

'Calm down,' Madam Green said, 'and start from the beginning.'

Elven took a deep breath and began telling her about the men. As she listened, Madam Green's usually calm face turned grim. Throwing down her gardening gloves, she told Elven to lead the way. Gogo, curious as always, tried to follow them and would not be persuaded to stay. In the end, Madam Green had to shut him inside the kennel.

'Can't he come along?' Elven asked as they hurried down the trail. 'He seems to know that something bad is happening.'

'That's precisely why he has to stay,' Madam Green said in a firm voice. 'Gogo can be overly protective when there's a threat. We can't have him charging at those men. Not till we find out more.'

They headed towards the creek in silence. Holding hands, they crossed the shallow part of the water on some moss-covered stones. Madam Green gestured for Elven to proceed slowly as they pushed their way through the bushes right to the edge of the mountainside. The sound of hammering floated up from below.

'Hydraulic miners, no doubt about it,' Madam Green said as they peered over the edge. In the barren pit below, Elven saw the four men she had seen earlier. But this time, they weren't just standing around talking. Two of the men were sawing up timber planks, while the other two were fixing them to the ground. 'Once they find gold, they won't stop.'

Elven suddenly remembered the painting in the Heritage Museum—the one with miners panning for gold. 'So it's true! There really is gold.'

'There was a gold rush thirty years ago. It's the reason why Armora exists. Many of the townsfolk are either miners who settled there or people who profited from the boom. In the beginning,' Madam Green continued, 'the miners were individuals panning the creek for gold nuggets. The tools they used were rudimentary—picks, shovels, and cast-iron pans to separate the gold from the earth. Later, someone invented the cradle—it was a wooden cot for rocking nuggets, not newborn babes. But then, everything changed with the water cannon.'

'I heard them talk about that!' Elven exclaimed. 'About clearing a bigger area and then using a nostril.'

'A *nozzle*.' Madam Green chuckled softly before her face grew stern again. 'It's an iron nozzle, a part of the equipment they use for hydraulic mining. What those men plan to do is to blast the mountainside with dynamite. After the surface rocks are loosened, they will pipe the creek's water into a canvas hose and out through the cannon. Now, you may not think it's much, but a large amount of water speeding through a narrow hose is enough to kill an ox!'

Elven sat down on the hard ground. 'Are they washing the gold out of the mountain?'

'Exactly. The jets of water will blast the side of the pit, dislodging the gold and rocks. The gold settles in the sluice because it's heavier, while the finer sand and mud don't get caught.'

'That must be the sluice.' Elven pointed to the long trough-like structure the men were building.

Madam Green nodded. 'Now where do you think the mud water goes after it exits the sluice?'

Elven frowned. 'Down?'

'Down where?'

'Down the mountain?'

'Down to the land around the mountain. Tons and tons of mud water flowing down like an unstoppable avalanche of muck and grime.' Madam Green stared down at the miners with sudden hatred. 'There used to be a small village right below this pit. I shall never forget the flood and the sight of those rice fields submerged in mud. Children were wading about in sludge that was up to their chests. An old woman died because she was too ill to get out of bed . . . That was what got the townsfolk up in arms. They formed protest groups and, with the help of some politicians, drove the miners out.'

'Then, we'll protest!' Elven said fiercely. 'We'll rally the townsfolk and stand up to those bad men!'

Madam Green sighed. 'The village never recovered from the flood. The damage was so devastating that everyone simply abandoned their homes and moved away.'

Elven thought of the happy times she had spent walking the dogs in the forest. The crunch of leaves underfoot and the soft carpet of moss on the rocks and boulders. The ferns that dotted the landscape like oversized feathers. Was this all going to end tomorrow when the men returned with their equipment? And what about the trees? What would they feed the parrots with if the men cut down all the fruit trees? Where would the forest animals and birds live?

'Once these men succeed, there'll be no stopping others from coming.' Madam Green's mouth hardened into a thin line. 'What do you think will happen if they start mining on the southern side of the mountain, right above Armora?'

The thought was terrifying. 'We have to alert the police chief immediately. He'll arrest them!'

'It's not as simple as that,' Madam Green said. 'To this day, there are no laws banning mining on the mountain itself. Which means the chief has no authority to stop them.'

'But we have to do something!' Elven said. 'We can't let them destroy an entire town!'

Madam Green did not reply but her eyes were shining with a steely determination.

They crept away from the edge and wandered around the creek's bank, racking their brains for ideas. Elven thought they might get the Armorians to form a human barricade but Madam Green shook her head. 'They won't care,' was all she would say about them. They tossed up one idea after the next but nothing seemed the least feasible. At sunset, after the miners had cleared out, they headed back to the empty pit to inspect the damage. To their dismay, a large section of the sluice had been completed. They took in the long wooden gutter in silence. How ugly it looked, snaking across the dirt like a serpent!

'Fast workers,' Madam Green muttered.

'What do we do?' Elven asked. 'They'll be back for the trees tomorrow.'

'I don't know, dear. I'm trying to think.'

Elven collapsed with her back against a tree trunk. 'Oh, I wish the mountain witch would just scare them off!'

'Right, the scary mountain witch.' Madam Green gave an exasperated sigh. 'No doubt described to you in vivid details by an Armorian?'

'Everyone knows about her,' Elven said, recalling Harris' words.

Madam Green gave her a withering look. 'There are no witches.'

'Then, why does everyone talk about her?'

'Have you seen anybody flying around on a broomstick?'

'No, but they say—'

'Whatever you've been hearing,' Madam Green snapped, 'it's not true.'

Elven crossed her arms and turned away. She was too tired to argue. They sat apart, steaming in their own indignation until Madam Green finally broke the awkward silence.

'I don't know about you,' she said, 'but I can't think straight if I'm hungry. Let's head back for supper. Maybe a good idea will come up after we eat.'

Elven accepted the olive branch with a harrumph.

'I suppose that's a yes, Miss Grumpy?'

Elven gave her a grudging smile. There was no way she could be mad at Madam Green for long. Standing up, Elven made her way across the pit.

Suddenly, she heard a loud shriek. 'You're bleeding!' Madam Green cried, running up to her.

Twisting her neck, Elven realized that the back of her flour sack dress was wet with what looked like blood. She gasped and lost her footing, stumbling against Madam Green.

'Don't move.' Madam Green steadied her by the arm. Then, as if she were peeling off the skin of an overly ripe plum, she lifted up the back of Elven's soggy shirt. 'There are large patches of red stains between your shoulder blades,' Madam Green said, pressing her fingers lightly against Elven's back. 'Does this hurt?'

Elven shook her head.

'How odd. Your skin's perfectly fine. No wounds or anything.' Madam Green peered back at her in puzzlement. 'Wait!' she cried, sprinting back to the tree where they had been standing. She stared at the trunk for a split second before collapsing in hysterical laughter.

'What's the matter?' Elven shouted, running over.

'It's not blood,' Madam Green said, in between chuckles. 'It's only the sap of the vampire tree.'

'Vampire!'

Madam Green smiled and wiped away the tears from her eyes. 'It's just a name,' she said, pointing to the large tree. From between the cracked bark, streams of thick red liquid were oozing down the tree trunk. 'These are very rare trees that grow on Mount Armora. They "bleed" only once every ten years, usually in the heat of summer. I've heard my mother talk about them when I was a little girl, but this is the first time I'm seeing it with my own eyes.'

Madam Green fumbled in her apron and produced a pocket knife. Flicking the blade open, she stuck it into the next tree. She twisted and scraped the soft bark, which began to crumble off the trunk, revealing a damp layer of wood inside. Madam Green buried her blade in and jiggled it hard. There was a tiny gurgle before crimson sap burst through the incision. Staining the blade a dark reflective red, it trickled down the trunk and into the soil.

Elven stuck her index finger into the red sap, which was just a touch more viscous than real blood. She shuddered.

'Why do they bleed?' she asked as she wiped her finger on a moss-coated rock. The red stain remained, stubborn as a wart.

'Nobody knows. But look, they are practically surrounding the pit.'

'Oh no! We can't have the miners felling them.'

'No, that'll be—' Madam Green stopped abruptly in mid-sentence, her eyes fixed unblinkingly at the vampire trees. '—excellent . . .'

'What?'

'I have an idea.' Madam Green turned to Elven with a cryptic smile. 'And it's really creepy.'

16

Revelations in the Dark

That evening, after a quick dinner slapped together from leftovers, Madam Green and Elven changed out of their floral skirts and put on black trousers and headscarves. Taking a kerosene lamp with them, they made their way down the mountain. In Armora, digging through the bins dotted around town, they amassed a dozen cracked glass jars and old newspapers, which they stuffed into their hemp bags.

As they passed by an inn, they heard a loud commotion from within. Peeking in through the window, Elven saw three of the miners sprawled on the floor with empty mugs around them, singing at the top of their lungs. A waiter was grabbing their arms, shouting for them to get up. But any effort to move the drunkards was met with rowdy resistance and raucous laughter.

'It's wonderful that they're drunk,' Madam Green said. 'They most likely won't head up the mountain until late in the morning or until after lunch. That'll buy us more time.'

'Maybe we ought to feed their mules some wine too . . .'

Madam Green laughed. 'That might work temporarily.'

'So what exactly are we doing?' Elven asked for the umpteenth time that night.

'All will be revealed, child.' Madam Green suddenly looked thoughtful. 'But you've just given me another idea. I'll pop by the chemist before we head home.'

'The chemist is open at this hour?'

'Not really.' Madam Green tightened the black scarf around her head. 'But he's an old friend and he'll let me in. Now, why don't you wait here and keep an eye on them?' With that, she hurried down Main Street, leaving Elven to guard the hemp sacks outside the inn window.

Elven's skin crawled as she watched the man called Skunk throw up on the floor. Then, in an attempt to stand up, Skunk grabbed the leg of a passing barmaid. The poor girl screamed and cursed. As she struggled to free herself, the beer in her hands splashed onto the faces of the nearby patrons. Skunk's men bawled in laughter and flung their empty glasses against the wall in merriment. A scuffle broke out as two of the customers who got drenched tried to punch Skunk in the face. But Skunk was built like a bull, with arms as thick as legs of ham. The poor townsfolk did not stand a chance. The other patrons swore and heckled but no one else was brave enough to challenge a man like that, especially when he had been emboldened by alcohol.

The front door of the inn burst open, causing Elven to jump. A short stout figure dashed out, followed by a woman. Before they could see her, Elven had ducked around the corner.

'No, dear, calm down!' cried the woman tugging at the man's sleeve. It was hard to see their faces clearly in the dark but Elven guessed from their movements that they were probably middle-agers.

'Don't tell me to calm down!' the man shouted back. 'The nerve of those scoundrels! Humiliating me on *my* property!'

'Best not to offend them. We don't want trouble from Gordon.'

'Shush!' The innkeeper glanced around. Not seeing Elven crouched among the shadows, he carried on softly. 'I don't understand it. A man of his stature getting mixed up with such lowlifes . . .' The innkeeper stared at the stable behind the inn before adding grimly, 'It's not right, keeping young ones locked up like that.'

'We have to be careful, dear,' the innkeeper's wife said. 'Please, just grin and bear with it for one more night.'

The innkeeper nodded. His wife put her hand on his arm and they headed back inside.

Once she made sure the street was empty, Elven crawled back out of the shadows. Were there children locked in the stable like horses and donkeys? She paced about, glancing at the stable until her curiosity finally got the better of her. Who were they? She had to at least take a look.

Elven hid the hemp bags in the bushes and headed towards the large, unfinished structure. Its entrance was shielded by a large, flat sheet of corrugated metal hanging off a horizontal wooden pole.

What can the miners possibly want with these children?

There was only one way to find out. Heart thumping, Elven gave the metal sheet a push. It let out an awful creak but slid open just wide enough for her to squeeze in. The stench of urine was overpowering. Holding her nose, she stepped into the dim interiors.

There were two rows of stalls on either side of the stable. Through the open window in the back wall, she could see the setting sun disappearing behind a distant line of trees. She ventured down the aisle between the stables and felt the crunch of hay beneath her threadbare soles. The place was unfit even for animals. The stalls she passed looked like they were falling apart.

She paused, uncertain whether to carry on. In the silence, she heard the drip-dripping of water from the roof. No, she must have heard wrong. It was impossible that a human could live in such conditions. As she turned to go, Elven heard a sudden scraping of heavy metal behind her. Something jumped out from the darkness and grabbed her shoulder. She let out a scream, but a hand shot out and clamped tight over her mouth.

'Quiet!' a hoarse voice whispered. The grip on her mouth tightened.

Elven gagged at the muddy stench of her captor.

'I won't hurt you,' the voice rasped. 'Help me, please?'

Elven nodded, her stomach churning. The grip around her relaxed. Without a moment's hesitation, Elven swung her elbow back and hit her captor in the ribs.

'Owww!' the foul creature cried, stumbling back.

Elven sprang away in repulsion. When she turned back, she saw, to her surprise, that he was just a boy. His hair was matted and dry. And it was hard to tell under the dim light what he was wearing under that layer of caked mud.

'What did you do that for?' Thick dust buffeted the slanting rays from the window as the skinny lad straightened up with a growl.

Elven took a step back. 'Stay away from me,' she threatened, 'or I'll . . . I'll—'

A look of recognition flashed across the boy's dirty face. His mouth fell open.

'Blimey!' he cried. 'Elv? Is it really you?'

17

The Moles

'Coal . . .?' Elven gasped. Blood rushed to her cheeks. Nobody called her Elv except her best friend.

'Holy moly!' she shouted, throwing herself at him. Coal let out a yelp as they tumbled against a stack of straw bales.

'Sorry, sorry!' Elven untangled herself, her cheeks burning. She was surprised by how easily she had overpowered Coal. This was a boy who had once handled flour sacks like they were filled with cotton. How weak he had become!

'Golly, you really made it here,' she exclaimed, sitting up.

'In a way, I guess.'

'You won't believe the adventures I've had since I left the orphanage,' Elven continued, her eyes shining. 'Do you remember Master Takuno, the person who made my Puzzle Box? Well, he's passed away. So now, I have to find the Key myself.'

'I'm not sure I follow you . . .'

'Don't worry! I'll explain everything once we get you cleaned up. And I know just the place.' Elven sprang to her feet. 'How do you fancy a trip up Mount Armora?'

'I can't go with you.' Coal's features twisted into bitterness.

'Of course you can.' Elven extended him her hand. 'Come on!'

'You don't understand,' he insisted. 'I'm a little tied up at the moment.'

It was only when Coal struggled to sit up that she saw the thick iron chain clamped around his left ankle. A sickening realization hit her.

'The miners . . . they did this to you?' Elven asked through gritted teeth.

'You've seen them?' His voice was shaky.

'That's why I'm here . . . to stop them from destroying Mount Armora. That fellow, Skunk, he's real nasty.'

'Director Hammond's a saint next to them.'

'And Mrs Monteiro a fairy godmother.'

The thought of the head caretaker in a fluffy taffeta gown complete with wings and a wand made them both grin. Elven knelt down to examine the metal piece around Coal's leg. 'The clasp's too snug, but the chain links don't look too strong,' she said. 'Maybe we can pry them apart.'

Coal's gaunt cheekbones protruded unhappily as he tried to say something. But Elven had already stood up, scanning the room for a tool she could use. She spotted a stall fork resting against a far wall. Maybe that would do the trick.

'Ain't going to work,' Coal called out in a listless voice as she ran to grab it.

'You never know till you try!' Elven said, kicking up dust and hay as she ran back to him. 'One weak link is all we need.' She forced a smile as she twisted the fork's prongs against the chain.

'You're very stubborn,' Coal said.

'Something I learned from you,' Elven teased. On the inside, though, she was torn to shreds. Coal had always been her protector, her guardian. Now that their roles were reversed, she couldn't let him down.

'So, tell me,' she asked in a bid to distract him, 'how did you end up here?'

Coal's face tightened. 'It all happened the night after you left. I crept back to the kitchen, hoping for a chance to return to my room. But Director Hammond was already there waiting for me. I tried to delay them so that you'd have time to get away. But when Hammond eventually realized the truth, he was so furious he . . . he punched me and knocked me out cold.'

'The monster!' Elven cried, twisting the fork against the clasp on Coal's leg.

Coal let out a yelp.

'Sorry!' Elven removed her headscarf and stuffed it between the metal and Coal's ankle to protect his skin. 'Go on,' she said, ignoring the dubious look on his face as she resumed the twisting motion.

'When I came to in the morning, I was tied against the flagpole. I felt a glass being pressed against my lips. "Drink," a man said and I did . . . not caring if it was poison. My head was throbbing so bad I felt I was going to die. "Now why did you go do that for, lad?" the man asked after I'd drunk my fill. For a moment, I thought they had caught you, and that he was a policeman coming to put me behind bars. But he said that they hadn't been looking for you. Apparently, nobody had run away before and Hammond had no idea what to do. He thought you'd probably give up and come back.'

'Go back to that place?' Elven scoffed. 'But wait, will they let you go if I return? If it means turning myself in—'

'It's nothing like that,' Coal said, his voice curt. He eyed the stall fork and shook his head. 'It's no use. Even if you can free me, you can't stop them.'

'But—'

Coal stood up abruptly and limped towards the back of the barn. Elven followed, wondering how he had injured his leg.

A long, wooden cage on wheels stood in the corner, partially covered by a muddy piece of canvas. By the fading light, Elven made out five small figures huddled next to one another. For a moment, a horrible thought crossed her mind: *They can't be dead, can they?* Then, one of them coughed, and she saw to her relief that their chests were rising and falling with their breaths.

'I'm supposed to take care of them, but I can't—' Coal's voice broke and he swiped at his eyes. 'They don't even give us enough water.'

Elven stared at the children in silence. There were three boys and two girls. The two sleeping with their faces turned to her looked Mawoli with their black hair and dark skin.

'Who are they?' Elven whispered.

'They're Ariki and Anika—Mawoli siblings from the Southland,' Coal said. 'Their parents were accused of stealing chickens and were sentenced to ten years in prison.'

Elven's mouth fell open. 'Ten years? Must have been a lot of chickens.'

'Just two. They tell me the sentence is twice as long because they're Mawolis.'

Elven pointed to the other three children. 'And who are they?'

Coal's eyebrows shot up. 'Don't you recognize Ryan, Matthew, and Ginger?'

'Ryan . . . Ginger?' Elven repeated, her voice cracking. 'From the orphanage? But that's impossible . . .'

She reached out and touched the boy through the bars. A faint crease flitted between his brows but he barely stirred.

'Ryan, wake up!' Elven cried, shaking him by his foot.

'It's no use. The men force this drink on them after dinner. Knocks them out cold. No way they can escape at night, you see?' Coal reached the cage and tucked a thin, sodden blanket over the children's bodies. 'They don't give it to me so I can take care of the others.'

'But they're supposed to be in a boarding school! They've won the scholarships!'

'There isn't a boarding school, Elv.' Coal's face darkened. 'We were tricked.'

Tricked? She tried to make sense of what Coal was saying, but all she could think of was the animated discussion she overheard in the staff lounge the day she ran away. 'But Morodon-Gore . . . that was the name of the headmaster. He was in there, remember? They didn't make him up!'

'Of course I remember,' Coal said, his eyes flashing. 'Morodon-Gore was the man who untied me from the flagpole. He said he admired my guts—sweet-talker that he was—and offered me a job at the boarding school.'

'And Director Hammond let you leave?'

'Why wouldn't he?' Coal snorted. 'One less troublemaker to take care of. But Morodon-Gore had us all fooled. After we left, he drove us straight to a gold mine where Ginger and I spent weeks hauling dirt and crushing rocks under the hot sun. You should have seen Ginger. Her skin was peeling like a snake the whole time. But we were lucky. Ryan and Matthew were sent underground with the Mawoli kids—they were small enough to move along the shafts . . .' Tears filled Coal's eyes, and he wiped them away with his raggedy sleeve. 'They treated them like rats . . . like—'

'Moles,' Elven whispered, giving Coal's arm a squeeze. 'They're bringing you up Mount Armora tomorrow, aren't they?' She finally understood what the miners had meant. 'Are the keys with Skunk?' Elven asked as she tested the padlock on the cart.

Coal nodded.

Elven frowned. 'I have to find help.'

'No.' Coal grabbed her hand, his voice suddenly fierce. 'Morodon-Gore is well-connected in Armora. I've heard the miners say so. I don't know who he really is, but he's powerful. He could very well be in cahoots with the authorities.'

'My friend Madam Green has a plan to save Mount Armora,' Elven said. 'I'm sure she'll think of a way to free you—'

'It's too dangerous,' Coal protested. 'Besides, there's nothing you can do tonight. Not with the kids asleep—'

Just then, a metallic screech cut through Coal's words. The stable door slid open. Coal's eyes widened with panic as he pulled Elven away from the cart and into the nearest stall.

'You kids still jabbering, eh?' a gruff male voice slurred in the dark. 'I'll pour a pint of beer down your throat, that's what I'll do, haha.'

'No, sir!' Coal shouted. 'It's just me talking to myself, sir!'

'You're an idiot, boy! The boss needs you all in top shape tomorrow. So, shut up or I'll give you a walloping you'll never forget!'

'Yes, sir! I'll go right to sleep, sir!'

The stable door closed with a screech and bang. Coal grabbed Elven's hand and pulled her over to the open window in the back wall.

'Go!' he whispered, pushing her out. 'And don't come back.'

18

Of Bugs and Lies

Elven found Madam Green standing outside the inn with a worried expression on her face. It was quickly replaced by shock, though, when she learned about the kidnapped children.

'We have to help them,' Elven pleaded.

'We will help them, I promise,' Madam Green said in a low voice. 'Just not tonight. We need to carry out our plan and we're running out of time.'

'But what's this plan of yours?' Elven cried. 'Why won't you tell me anything?'

'When we get home, we're going to make bug traps.'

'That's it? The two of us against the four of them, and all we have are bug traps?'

Madam Green pursed her lips. 'It's just bug traps for now.' And that was all she would say as she left Elven stewing in her own thoughts all the way up Mount Armora.

It was close to nine when they reached the house. Once inside, Madam Green headed straight to the stove and began cooking sugar syrup in a saucepan. Elven was given the task of cleaning and washing the jars they had collected in town. When this was done, they sat down and rolled up paper funnels from pieces of newspapers. After the syrup had cooled down, Elven poured it into the jars, which Madam Green capped with the paper funnels.

'Now can you tell me how we're going to save the children?' Elven demanded, unable to hold in her curiosity any longer.

'I'm trying to catch enough creepy-crawlies to make a proper bug paste,' Madam Green said, heading outside with a tray full of traps.

'But what has that got to do with stopping the miners?' Elven asked, trailing behind Madam Green as she placed the jars around the garden. 'Are we smearing it on their faces when they're drunk?'

Madam Green burst out in laughter. 'Oh, my word. I doubt those men would succumb to such a beauty treatment.' She rubbed her eyes with the back of her hand and stifled a yawn. 'Golly, it's late. We ought to go to bed soon. You have a special task tomorrow and I need you to be in top form.'

'What task?'

Madam Green sat down on the garden bench, her tired face suddenly alert under the moonlight. 'Have you ever lied to anyone, Elven?'

Elven drew in a sharp breath. Madam Green's gaze was like a spear penetrating her skull. She wondered if the older woman had seen something bad in her.

Something she, too, was unaware of. Maybe she knew that Elven wasn't Mavarian.

'I've lied in the orphanage. I was desperate . . . and I'm not proud of it.' She hung her head, afraid of what Madam Green would see. 'Does this mean I'm not good enough for the task?'

'No, darling, of course not.' Madam Green reached out and raised Elven's chin. 'Besides, anyone would have lied in your circumstances.'

The tension seeped out of Elven's body. 'Thank you,' she muttered. What was it about the older woman that always made her feel like a better person?

'Do you remember the clearing with the midnight horrors trees?' Madam Green asked.

'The trees with the long dangling seed pods? Near where we pick our wild bananas?'

Madam Green nodded. 'We have to direct the miners to the Midnight Horrors Grove tomorrow.' Her face was solemn. 'To do that, we need to put aside our "morals" for a while. You see, they need to set up camp there so that we can do a little painting . . .'

Elven's eyes grew wide with excitement as Madam Green proceeded to outline her plan. A plan that was built on a great, big lie. And, in order to execute it, Elven had to be a tarantula that could spin a web of deceit and swallow her prey without remorse.

Elven thought back to the times when she had lied at the orphanage. Like the day she had finished cleaning the staff lounge in twenty minutes but said it took thirty because she was secretly dancing to the music from the gramophone. And she had always told everyone that her baby spoon was made of pure silver. Of course it wasn't—the last time she checked, it remained as untarnished as ever, marking it steel. Maybe the spoon wasn't even hers. Maybe someone was finishing up a cup of tea en route depositing her at the orphanage when the dastardly teaspoon had fallen into the basket. Still, these were thoughts best kept to herself.

So, it wasn't completely true that she lied only when she was desperate.

In fact, I've become quite the clever liar, Elven realized with sudden shame. *What will Madam Green think of me if she sees how cunning I am?*

'I can do all the talking if this makes you uncomfortable,' Madam Green said, interrupting her thoughts. 'I know I'm asking a lot of you.'

'It's not that . . . In fact, I think I ought to go alone.'

'Alone?' Madam Green's forehead crumpled between her finely arched eyebrows. 'But you're only a child.'

In the darkness, Gogo let out a low growl, as if sensing her uncomfortable thoughts.

'They won't hurt a child.' The words sounded hollow as they left Elven's mouth but she added, 'Besides, I'm too tall to be enslaved as a Mole.'

'So is Coal, my dear.'

'But if I'm the only one leading them to the grove then you'll have a chance to snoop around when we're gone. Someone's got to find the key to the cage.'

Madam Green sighed but said nothing.

'So, I can go by myself, can't I?' Elven persisted.

'I suppose you have a point,' Madam Green conceded to Elven's surprise. 'It's possible they'll trust the words of a child more than those of an adult . . .'

She gazed up at the full moon, her expression unreadable. 'Fine,' she said, fixing her eyes back on Elven. 'You can go alone, but on one condition: You must take Gogo with you. And if anything goes wrong, you set Gogo on them, and you run.'

'But won't they hurt Gogo?'

'Gogo knows how to take care of himself.'

'I'll be fine.' Elven gave the older woman's hand a squeeze. Madam Green's palm reminded her of a warm slab of stone. It was a working woman's hand, the hand of someone who had probably grown up on a farm. 'Gogo will make sure I'm fine.'

The wrinkles around Madam Green's mouth tightened ever so slightly. 'First thing tomorrow, we'll go over your lines.'

19

When the Tree Bleeds

The next morning, Elven, Madam Green, and Gogo parked themselves at the edge of the clearing nearest to the pit. They waited for a long time before Skunk's wagon finally appeared along the mountain trail, kicking up clouds of dust in its wake. Rounding the bend, the two-mule wagon gave a resigned groan before screeching to a stop at the clearing. This time, there was only the bald man with Skunk.

'Get moving! Work off your booze!' Skunk landed with a thud on the grass, his mean voice reverberating through the cool mountain air. 'No time to waste!' he shouted, banging his spade against the side of the wagon to make his point.

'You're not helping my headache,' the bald man groaned.

'And you're not helping much,' Skunk snapped. He was about to launch into a tirade when a horse-drawn cage driven by Moldylocks appeared around the bend.

'Seems like my little helpers have arrived!' Skunk said, sounding pleased.

Elven looked on in dismay as Moldylocks pulled up next to the wagon.

'Ladies and gentlemen, I present to you . . .' Skunk strode up to the cage, his arm raised in a theatrical gesture. 'The lovely Moles!'

He ripped off the canvas like a magician revealing his trick and burst into laughter. Blinded by the sudden sunlight, the children cowered against the opposite side of the cage, their arms raised in fear. Skunk ran his spade against the wooden bars, cackling like a madman.

'Stop!' Elven hissed between clenched teeth. How could anyone be so cruel?

Although he was just one man, Skunk's energy seemed to be that of ten. Here, he was barking orders for them to get out, and there he was deftly unhitching the mules from the wagon. His men, in contrast, looked bored and tired as they saddled the animals with baskets of tools.

Skunk sauntered ahead, whistling as he led the first mule across the creek. In a line, the children waded across the water, followed by the men with heavy sacks slung across their shoulders and the second mule.

'Come on now,' Madam Green whispered, and they crept along the undergrowth, careful to keep some distance. Gogo seemed reluctant to follow them—perhaps he had a bad feeling about the miners.

Once in the pit, the children were given orders to unload the equipment while the men stood about under the shade of trees, listless as fat cats in a hot spell. If Skunk was offended by their lack of enthusiasm, he did not show it. Instead, he strode around with a can of white paint, marking the trees to be felled. As soon as he was done, Skunk tossed the can aside and reached into the mule's basket for an axe. Slowly but deliberately, he advanced towards the first line of trees closest to the creek.

'Come on now,' Elven whispered. 'Sink it in deep.'

Gogo, who was crouched beside her, whined. Elven quickly covered his muzzle for fear of being found out.

Thwack! The blade made contact with the tree. Elven pulled Gogo close, her entire body rigid.

Thwack! Thwack!

There was silence, then a dull thump as the heavy axe hit the grass.

'Argh! What in the world?!'

Elven looked up in time to see Skunk staggering away from the tree, his face and body splattered with red sap. She grabbed Madam Green's hands, barely able to contain her excitement. What sweet revenge!

Skunk let loose a chain of expletives as he held up his 'bloody' hands. The men's mouths fell open.

'What in the devil's name is this?' Skunk demanded as a gob of sap dripped down his brows. He wiped his sleeve across his face, and a comical band of red appeared across his eyes. The men chuckled but quickly shut their mouths at his growl of displeasure.

'Calm down, Skunk,' Moldylocks said, grinning. 'No need to . . . see red.'

Like a wild beast, Skunk lunged at Moldylocks. The two of them stumbled against a tree and fell, kicking at each other in the dirt. The bald man sprang to intervene, but Skunk had already let go of Moldylocks. His eyes were fixed on the tree in pure horror. A thick piece of bark had fallen to the ground from behind Moldylocks' head and red liquid was spluttering and squirting from the tree.

Moldylocks screamed and scrambled away. 'It's alive!' He shook his hair, sending the red liquid flying this way and that. 'I felt a pulse! A freaking pulse!'

'I don't like the look of that,' said the bald man. 'Makes your hair stand.' He backed away from Moldylocks and Skunk, his face stricken with terror.

'This is it,' Madam Green whispered to Elven. 'Lead them to the grove and keep them there for as long as you can. I will see you back at the house.' She gave Elven's hand a squeeze. 'Good luck!'

Elven nodded. Tugging Gogo's leash, she crawled away from the creek's edge until she was close to the mountain trail. Checking again to make sure she was unobserved, she got up and brushed the leaves from her dress.

Then, steeling herself, she began to sing. Her voice was hoarse in the beginning, but as she made her way across the clearing, it grew loud and clear. As expected, when she came into view, the men were staring warily in her direction.

'Good afternoon!' she shouted across the creek, pretending to be surprised.

'What are you doing here, girl?' barked the bald man. 'Are you from the town?'

'Yes, sir. I'm walking my dog,' replied Elven, in the brightest tone she could muster. 'We love the fresh mountain air. Are you out camping?'

'Camping?' Skunk stepped out from behind the men and bared his teeth at her. 'Do I look like a happy camper?'

Elven faked a shriek, which startled Gogo so much that he started barking. In the distance, she saw that the children were murmuring among themselves. Matthew started pointing at Elven, but his hand was quickly slapped away by Coal.

'It's all right, little girl,' said the bald man. 'Some tree spat blood on him, that's all. Nothing to be afraid of.'

'Good heavens!' Elven cried. 'I pray you didn't cut the vampire trees, sir?'

'What's that?' asked the bald man, alarmed.

'You from out of town?' Elven asked innocently.

'Yes, we're tree surgeons from the city.' The bald man flashed a nervous smile at her. 'Now, come over here and tell us about these vampire trees.'

So far so good. 'It's bad luck to cut the sacred trees,' she said, making her way across the creek on the smooth flat rocks. 'Very bad luck.'

The men's eyes fell on Skunk.

'Sacred trees?' Skunk frowned. 'There's no such thing as sacred trees.'

Elven clicked her tongue. 'That's what the old miner said when they told him not to touch the trees.'

'What miner?' Skunk asked, suddenly interested. 'Tell me. And you'd better not be fibbing.'

Elven's fingers tightened around the leash. Skunk looked real mean. If she didn't get the story right, she could be in big trouble. She pulled Gogo close for strength.

'I didn't make anything up. My mother herself told me this,' she protested with a scowl. 'The trees on this mountain have spirits living in them. If you make a tree bleed, you're cursed forever. During the gold rush, there was a miner who didn't believe this. He cut down the trees to look for gold. He even laughed when he made the trees bleed. When the townsfolk warned him to stay away, he called them superstitious.

'But the spirits were angry, and they haunted him. For thirteen days and thirteen nights, creatures of the forest visited him and sucked on his flesh until even the lepers shunned him. The old miner begged and swore, but he could not drive them away. When he tried to wash away the open sores on his body, they rotted deeper. Finally, even his ligaments fell off his bones like shredded cloth. There was nothing he could do to stop the bleeding. Nothing he could apply to numb the pain. Everything he ate soon tasted like blood and vomit. The miner was soon driven out of the town because everyone was afraid of his curse. Nobody wanted to be tainted.

'In the end, they found him drowned in a pond, which remained as red as blood until his body was fished out and dealt with.' Elven stopped and turned her face to Skunk slowly. 'And that is why nobody touches this mountain. Nobody.'

For a brief moment, she thought she saw Skunk's lips quiver. But before she could continue, the flicker of fear in his cold blue eyes was extinguished by scorn.

'Do you believe this stupid story?' Skunk turned to the men with a smirk. 'I mean, this is the stupidest story I've ever heard.'

'Old wives' tales and superstitions!' sneered the bald man. 'Look at this man here. Ain't he standing tall and strong? Your mother is foolish for filling your head with this nonsense, little girl. *My* mother, if she were alive, would have whipped me for spouting such fibs.'

Moldylocks guffawed and started to walk away. 'Get back to work,' he shouted at the children who had wandered out of the pit. 'Now!'

The children shuffled back reluctantly. Even without meeting their eyes, Elven could feel their desperation radiating to her. Her plan was slipping out of control. She had to do something quickly.

'Wait!' Elven shouted. 'My mother cut the bark of a vampire tree when she was pregnant with me.'

The miners turned and eyed her warily.

'And she's alive and well?' asked Moldylocks.

Elven did not answer but raised her left hand.

The six fingers said it all.

The men glanced at Skunk, then at Elven uncertainly. Nobody said a thing. Even the mountain seemed to be holding its breath.

'Come on, lads, it's just a coincidence,' Skunk said, breaking the silence. He picked up the axe and held it out to them. 'Get started on the other trees while I go wash up in the creek.'

The men grunted but did not move.

'It's true,' said a voice, coming to her rescue. Coal stepped out from the group of children, his eyes wide. 'It's taboo to cut vampire trees.'

Elven had avoided looking at the children for fear of arousing the miners' suspicions. But she could not help but stare at Coal now. What had been inconspicuous in the dark jumped out at her in their full horror. He was covered in bruises, sores, and cuts.

'Mawoli *tapu*,' squeaked the Mawoli boy, looking terrified. 'In our culture, *tapu* is inviolable. Otherwise, death!'

'What's this?' Skunk demanded. 'A rebellion?'

The children shrunk back.

'I ain't touching those trees,' the bald man said suddenly. His hands were buried defiantly in his pockets. 'I don't know about the rest of you but I'd rather be safe than sorry.'

'Aye, can't we just skip the tree-cutting and go straight to the creek?' asked Moldylocks, still staring at Elven's hand. 'Little girl, you don't think I'll be cursed just because he pushed me against a vampire tree, do you? Ain't my fault I scraped the bark.'

Elven stepped back, faking a grimace.

'I'll be surprised if the blood ain't poisonous,' the bald man added in a gloomy voice.

'Shut up!' Skunk flung the axe onto the grass. 'First of all, this ain't blood! It's just plain old tree sap! Where are we going to pitch our tents if we don't cut down the bloody—I mean sappy—trees? How are we going to work if we don't clear the bushes? You tell me!'

'I'm sick of your yelling! And you stink like your name!' The bald man jabbed his index finger at Skunk. 'Think you're better than us?'

'Yeah? So what? You're nothing but a superstitious fool!'

'Well, good riddance to you lot!' the bald man yelled. 'Let's see who's got the last laugh.' Throwing one last glance at the vampire tree, he stomped down the mountain trail, leaving the rest gaping.

'Go on, then!' Skunk shouted after the retreating silhouette, his face growing redder by the minute. 'Coward!'

'You might not want to set up camp here,' Elven said.

Skunk took a step towards her but stopped when Gogo let out a low growl. 'And why not, Miss Know-It-All?' he asked testily.

'The fire ants make their nests here. I usually camp in a spot that's further up. It's closer to the water too,' Elven said. 'I'll show you where if you give me a coin.'

Skunk thought hard for a moment.

'You lot,' he said, pointing to the children. 'Get into the cart. NOW!'

Elven watched as the group scrambled across the creek. Ryan had lost so much weight his trousers were hardly staying on his hips. Ginger barely resembled her former self, and Matthew had a horrible wheeze that seemed to worsen with each breath.

'Why do they have to go in there?' Elven blurted out, her emotions getting the better of her.

Skunk fixed an icy stare at her. 'None of your business,' he said, enunciating each word with slow menace.

Feeling the tension, Gogo barked. Elven tightened her grip on the leash and took a step back.

'Come on now, kids!' Moldylocks called out, shooing the staring children into the cart. 'We ain't got all day!'

Skunk fixed another look at Elven, then stomped across the water towards the cart. It was only when Elven reached out to pat Gogo on the head that she realized her hands were shaking. She put her feet on the wet stones, taking long, slow breaths with each step to calm herself down.

You can do it, she said to herself over and over again. Around her, the water sloshed and lapped at her trembling feet.

After all the kids were back behind bars, Skunk pulled out a key strung around his neck and secured the padlock. Elven's heart fell. So much for Madam Green getting hold of the key.

When he was done, Skunk pulled out a copper coin from his pocket and tossed it at Elven.

'Go on, then,' he said.

Stealing one last look at Coal, Elven turned and led the men up the mountain.

20

Midnight Horrors

With the nightmarish story of the ill-fated miner fresh on their minds, it took very little to convince the two men to pitch their tents further up the mountain. Once her job was done, Elven hurried back to the house with Gogo. To her surprise, Madam Green was already there, waiting. The older woman rushed forward and embraced Elven, her face relaxing visibly, if only temporarily.

'You saw Skunk hang the key around his neck, didn't you?' Elven said, dejected. 'There's no way we can steal it from him.'

'Who says we need the key?' A sly smile stretched across Madam Green's face. 'The cart is not as sturdy as it looks. I've slipped the kids a small tool. If they can take turns prying the boards—'

'You think of everything!' Elven cried.

'Not everything,' Madam Green said, patting Elven's back. 'We'll definitely need to check on them again. Those poor kids, I doubt they can last much longer.'

Elven's face crumpled as she pulled away from Madam Green. 'Do you think we can get them out tonight?'

'We'll get them out as soon as possible, darling.' Madam Green gave Elven's shoulders a squeeze. 'I promise.' Then, noting the time, she frowned. 'Let's get started, though. We don't have much time before the midnight horrors bloom.'

They hurried off to the east side of the mountain where wild fruit trees grew in abundance. Elven found several plum trees, but it would be a few more weeks before they were ripe for the picking. They concentrated instead on filling their sacks with mulberries, crab apples, and bananas. By now, Elven was quite able to distinguish sweet, ripe fruits from tart, inedible ones. Where her eyes had once been blind to the marvels of the forest, they could now easily pick out the medicinal plants that were Mother Nature's gift to mankind.

It took nearly an hour and three bulging hemp sacks before Madam Green was finally satisfied with their harvest. Back in the kitchen, Elven cut and mashed the wild fruits into a sludgy, sweet paste, while Madam Green went outside to check on the bug traps. Overnight, swarms of beetles, ants, wasps, and other creepy-crawlies had made their way into the bottles. Most had drowned in the syrup but a few were still alive and struggling to find their way out.

Madam Green brought the traps inside, and very carefully she poured the bugs into the large bowl of fruit paste that Elven was mashing.

'Ewww!' Elven squealed as a groggy wasp crawled up her hand.

'Want to try some?' Madam Green held up a spoonful to her face. 'It's full of goodness.'

Elven squealed and jumped away.

'You don't know what you're missing,' Madam Green said with a laugh.

The kitchen darkened as a cloud passed over the sun. Elven looked out of the window at the grey and purplish sky.

'It looks like it's going to rain. Will that affect our plan?'

'Hopefully not, sweetheart,' Madam Green said as she stirred in some wild banana chunks. 'Hopefully not.'

* * *

That night, a silver moon peeked between the clouds, barely obscured by the curious-looking trees surrounding the clearing. The bases of their trunks were buried in piles of bone-like twigs while, above, long seed pods hung off the bare, spindly branches. When the wind blew, the trees shivered like an army of skeletons waving their daggers over their enemies' fallen corpses.

This was the grove of the midnight horror trees— the very spot where Elven had led the miners earlier in the day.

The night was hot and still, as if waiting for the sky to split open with rain. Elven sat in the bushes next to Madam Green, her skin lined with a thin film of sweat.

The fumes of cigarettes and urine wafted through the humid air, and Elven imagined these vapours as noxious fingers teasing her hair and staining her clothes brown.

Her apron pockets were heavy with tools, which dug into her flesh whenever she shifted position. Gnats buzzed around her face, and she would have liked to smack them, but the sound would have given her away. So, she pulled the collar of her dress over her nose and shook her head violently this way and that.

Madam Green, on the other hand, seemed to hardly notice the storm of gnats encircling them. Leaning lightly against the bucket of bug paste they had brought along, she sat as serene as a stone statue with her eyes closed and her legs crossed.

Inside the clearing, Skunk and Moldylocks were huddled around a fire, smoking, their voices low and indistinct. The horse by the tree stood still. A short distance away, the two mules had lain down on the ground. The children were quiet in their cage, except for bouts of coughing.

Time congealed into a thick stew of tobacco and sweat. Even the gnats lost interest in their little game of torment and finally left them in peace. To pass time, Elven tried to focus her thoughts on the Puzzle Box. An interesting idea came to her just as she was about to doze off. Master Takuno's Sales Journal contained his customers' surnames as well as the initials of their first names. Why not make a list of all the ones that could potentially be an anagram for YOU ARE MINE? It would be a mammoth task but not one that would be impossible. All she needed was time and patience, not unlike the way she perfected the seven shades of the rainbow cake. And, if she went back twelve years or so, there was a real possibility that she might even find the names of her parents!

A loud splash of water interrupted her thoughts, followed by a soft hiss as the campfire died down into glowing embers. The men stood up and trudged into their tent. The forest grew quiet, punctuated by the occasional hoot of an owl. Elven felt her companion's hand on her shoulder.

'Listen,' Madam Green whispered.

Elven cocked her head, then broke into a smile as she heard the sound they had been waiting for. Slowly and steadily, loudly and rhythmically, the men's snores punctuated the night air like the rattle of a broken machine. The miners were finally asleep!

They crawled out from under the bushes, pausing at the edge of the clearing until the moon was hidden by a passing cloud. Then, under the cover of darkness, they sprinted for the cart.

'Coal! Ginger! Did you manage to pry the—' Elven stopped, dumbfounded. All the children, with the exception of Coal, were asleep!

'Wake up!' she hissed, shaking the cart but the children barely registered her presence. Coal, on the other hand, was staring past her like she was invisible.

'The sleeping drug,' Elven uttered in disbelief. 'How are we going to get them out like this?'

Coal gazed at her blankly, his lids heavy.

'Coal! Listen to me!' She grabbed him hard. 'Did you take out the nails?'

'They made us drink . . .'

Good lord! They must have fed him the drug too!

'Got a board loose . . .' Coal muttered. 'Only one . . .'

'It's all right. I'll get you out.' Elven took out the pry bar from her apron pocket and placed it against one of the boards that formed the roof of the cage.

'Too tired . . .' Coal slumped over, his breath heavy.

'No, no, no!' Elven hit the cage with the pry bar. 'Don't go to sleep!'

'Quiet! Get a grip on yourself.' Madam Green snatched the pry bar away, her low voice laced with unease. 'We'll just have to come back for them tomorrow. Right now, we need to execute the plan.'

'But—'

'Even if we can pry open the roof, there's no way to carry all of them back to the house.'

'But we can push the cage into the forest.'

'And what? Hide them?'

'We can't leave them here! They'll die!'

'They *won't* die,' Madam Green said sternly. 'But if you don't help me, they may.'

Elven buried her face in her palms and let out a groan. But she knew Madam Green was right. Coal and the others would have to wait.

'We'll think of something,' Madam Green promised, pulling her away from the cart. 'Now help me. Please.'

Elven shot a last look at Coal, then followed Madam Green to the edge of the clearing. There, they hauled out the heavy bucket they had brought along and moved it next to the tent. Using wooden bowls, they scooped the paste out of the bucket and spread it over the top of the tarpaulin. As the mashed fruits and dead bugs dripped down, they worked quickly to distribute the sticky mixture with their paint brushes. Very soon, all sides of the tent were covered in a disgusting layer of bug paste. Madam Green gave Elven a thumbs-up.

'I should go in and look for the key,' Elven whispered.

'Are you out of your mind?'

Madam Green gripped Elven's arm and dragged her out of the clearing. She did not let go until they were safely hidden in a cluster of shrubs.

'But I feel bad,' Elven pleaded.

'So do I.' Madam Green's voice was soft but firm. 'There's nothing we can do right now.'

Elven felt as if she would cry, but there was no choice but to wait. They sat hidden for a while in silence until Madam Green asked, 'Can you see the midnight horrors blooming?'

Elven squinted through the foliage and shook her head. She hadn't really paid attention to the odd-looking flowers with their large, wrinkled petals. In fact, the flowers looked so crumpled, they almost seemed to be withering rather than blooming.

Madam Green took out a pocket watch and held it up under the moonlight. It was a quarter past ten. They continued to wait.

About thirty minutes passed, then an hour.

Then, a faint odour began to fill the air, getting stronger as time wore on. Elven sniffed and made a face.

'What's that awful smell?' she asked.

'That's the midnight horrors flowers.' Madam Green gave Elven's shoulder a squeeze. 'Be patient. The smell will bring them here.'

By midnight, the stench had grown unbearable. It was as if they were sitting in a heap of rotting meat and rat droppings. Still, nothing happened.

Just as Elven was about to doze off, she felt Madam Green shaking her. There was a soft flapping in the air, which grew louder by the second. Elven's hair stood on end as she felt the movement of a huge swarm of bats above their heads.

For a moment, they circled about the tent, their squeaks barely perceptible to Elven's ears. Then, without warning, the swarm launched itself against the tent. Flapping hysterically, the creatures sank their tiny teeth into the gooey mixture of wild fruits and insects.

The flimsy tent rattled and shook under the weight of the small furry bodies. A light came on inside the tent. They heard voices in various states of wakefulness and saw lumbering shadows.

'Go take a look!' Skunk's voice was muffled.

'Why me?' Moldylocks shot back.

'Get out there this instant!'

The bats did not care for Skunk's threats. All they knew was that the sweet, rotting paste was calling out to their long, agile tongues. They pounded the tent like hailstones, blood-curdling screams heightening the anticipation of their descent.

Suddenly, a drop of water fell on Elven's face. Another followed in quick succession, then another.

'Oh no,' Elven said.

'The bats have done their part,' said Madam Green, 'and the rain will help wash away any traces of the bug paste.'

'But the children will be drenched—'

'We have no choice,' Madam Green cut her off. 'Now, let's go before they find us.'

She pulled Elven to her feet and, together, they ran up the mountain trail towards the house. As they turned the corner over the rocky outcrop, a streak of lightning cracked the sky open, illuminating the entire landscape. Thunder boomed. The floodgates roared open. Elven turned and said a silent prayer for the children.

'Stay strong,' she muttered. 'I will be back for you.'

21

The Alchemist and the Brave

When Elven awoke, the sun was already high up in the sky. She jumped up and ran downstairs in her nightgown. In the kitchen, Madam Green was darning a pair of stockings at the table, like it was any other day.

'Did our plan work?' Elven asked. 'Are they gone?'

Madam Green looked up from her needlework, unruffled.

'Yes and no,' she said, 'Do you want some breakfast?'

'Never mind the breakfast!' Elven cried. 'Let's go and check on them now!'

'I already have. Moldylocks headed down the mountain this morning in the cart.'

Elven's face fell. 'And Skunk?'

'I'm afraid Skunk's still around.'

'So, it didn't work.' Elven collapsed into a chair.

'I wouldn't say that,' Madam Green replied. 'I do think he's spooked by our little trick. Otherwise he wouldn't have decamped from the grove. You should have seen the speed at which the wagon flew down to the riverbank this morning. I was surprised none of the children got thrown off the back!' She got up and scooped out a bowl of oatmeal from the saucepan. 'Here, I've saved you some.'

Elven stirred the creamy mixture listlessly, unable to work up an appetite. All she could think of was the children.

'We've failed,' Elven moaned.

'The war's not over yet!' Madam Green got the kettle down from the shelf and set it on the stove with a resounding clang. 'First, we'll have ourselves a strong cup of tea, then we'll make our next move.'

'Next move?' Elven leaped up, nearly upsetting her bowl. 'You have another plan?'

The corners of Madam Green's lips curled up into a half smile. 'I always have a plan.' She put on her mitts and opened the oven door. Very carefully, she took out a tray of white powder and placed it on top of the stove.

'Don't even think of tasting this,' Madam Green warned.

'Why? It's not—' A shiver ran up Elven's spine. '—poison, is it?'

'Let's just say it used to be baking powder,' Madam Green answered. 'Now eat your oatmeal.'

After breakfast, they went up to the rocky outcrop above the creek bend—a vantage point from which to observe both the pit and the wagon. Below them, Coal and Matthew were working on the sluice while the rest were assembling thick, black pipes. But without Skunk's henchmen to supervise them, their efforts looked chaotic and half-hearted.

Skunk himself was wandering about the pit like a lost soul. As he trudged past the vampire tree he had cut earlier, he paused and stared at it like a man possessed. Then, shaking his head, he moved on, mumbling to himself. He looked up from time to time, as if wary of someone or something watching him from behind the trees.

'It's like he's trying to decide if the curse is for real,' Elven said to Madam Green.

'You're probably right,' Madam Green replied, peering at him through her old opera glasses. 'His greed is calling out to him, but he's tired and scared.'

Elven took over the opera glasses. The mother of pearl casing on the twin tubes felt smooth and cool in her hands. She peered through them, searching the site until she found Coal and Matthew in the mid-section of the sluice. As he worked, Coal kept stealing glances around the pit, pretending to concentrate on his hammering only when Skunk turned his way.

'Coal's looking for me,' Elven said, suddenly hopeful. 'They must know we're nearby.'

Madam Green gave her a long, hard look. 'Are you sure you want to do this?' she asked.

Elven swallowed, remembering how Skunk had handled the patrons of the inn. But she took another glance down at the pit and nodded. 'You think it'll work?'

'I don't see why not,' Madam Green said. 'Look, he's only got his tools with him. Soon he'll be thirsty. And he'll need to get the rest of his things from the wagon. I'm pretty sure—'

Suddenly, her face fell and she choked on her words.

'What's wrong?' Elven asked in alarm.

Madam Green breathed out as she wiped her palm over her face. 'It's just . . . I feel bad that you have to be the one taking the risk. He recognizes you. I would do it myself, if not for the fact that you're nimbler and faster.'

'Your job's not any less dangerous, you know.'

'I just don't know what to do if he catches—'

'I won't be caught.' Elven rearranged her features into a smile. She had to be brave, for everyone's sake. 'Besides, I'll listen for your signal.'

Madam Green took out her bird whistle and blew. A melodious trill rang out, easing their heavy hearts for a brief moment. Then, Madam Green pulled out two glass vials from her pocket. One contained the white powder while the other was filled with clear liquid. She handed both vials to Elven.

'Their water should be in a metal jug with the lid,' she said. 'Remember, it's the liquid that goes into the water. Not the powder. That goes in Skunk's glass.'

'Don't worry,' Elven said. Inside, her heart was thumping. *What will I do if Skunk catches me?*

She shook the awful thought from her head. This was no time for doubt.

'Whatever happens,' Madam Green said, locking eyes with her, 'you have to keep moving.'

Elven nodded. Giving Madam Green a tight hug, she sprinted downhill along the soft, wet bank of the creek. Several times, she slipped and nearly fell. But soon, her feet had outrun her fears. In the distance, she saw the wagon, with the mules still hitched to it. She stopped to listen. All was quiet except for the rush of water.

Elven skipped across the creek with the sure-footedness of a mountain goat and sprinted for the wagon. Pulling herself up with one hand, she landed inside the wagon bed with a soft thud.

It took less than a second to spot the drinking jug. She lifted the metal container and felt the water slosh about inside. *Good*, she thought. Screwing its cap open, she emptied the liquid from her vial into it.

Now came the hard part. There were four glasses in the cart—which one did Skunk drink from? She stared at the glasses, paralyzed. It could be any one.

Plagued with indecision, Elven glanced back at the rocky outcrop where Madam Green was waiting. She knew that Madam Green would not blame her if she failed. But would she ever forgive herself?

A familiar twitter floated through the air—the bird whistle!

Elven gasped. Picking up three random glasses, she threw them into a sack next to her feet. Skunk wouldn't notice they were missing. Not as long as he had something to drink with.

The bird whistle sounded again, this time with urgency. Elven emptied the powder into the remaining glass and clambered over the side of the wagon. In her haste, her left foot hit the uneven grass at an awkward angle. Tears sprang to her eyes as she crumpled to the ground. She tried to stand up but a sharp pain shot through her ankle. Elven yelped and doubled over. She was done for. There was no way she could get away without being spotted.

Come on! yelled the voice in her head. *You didn't leave the orphanage to be a sitting duck!*

She threw herself down in the knee-high grass. With all the strength she could muster, she twisted and rolled her body until she was right under the wagon. Thank God she had her dark green overalls on!

A loud clatter rang out above her as something hit the wagon bed.

'Piece of junk!' Skunk cursed and gave the front wheel a kick. The mules whinnied and stomped their hooves in agitation.

'What now? Can't a man take a rest in his own wagon? Shut your traps, you stupid mules.' There was a loud thud above as he swung himself into the wagon.

Elven pressed herself flat against the ground and waited. What were her options? She could stay put and risk being found or she could make a run—or rather, a crawl—for those bushes a few yards away. She remembered what Madam Green had said:

'Whatever happens, you have to keep moving.'

Muttering a silent prayer, Elven rolled out from under the wagon and into a bed of tall bushy grass. Very slowly, she inched forward with her arms. Every movement felt like a noose loosening and tightening around her neck, every rustle of the grass an invitation to be found.

Elven was about to pull her legs into the bushes when she heard a loud noise from the wagon. She shut her eyes and waited for the inevitable. Any moment now and Skunk would be lifting her up with his paw-like hands.

A loud yawn punctuated the air.

Elven scooted into the bushes.

She raised her head inch by inch. Skunk was pacing around the wagon, a cigarette in hand. Elven watched as he exhaled long puffs of smoke into the air. His hunched shoulders made him seem older, less menacing. All of a sudden, a sneezing spell seized him. Skunk threw the cigarette away and wiped his nose and eyes with his sleeve. Muttering, he reached over into the wagon. A glass appeared in his hand. Skunk sneezed again and wiped his eyes.

'Go on,' Elven whispered.

Skunk grabbed the water jug and began pouring.

From where she was, Elven could see the chemical reaction perfectly. The clear clean water hit the bottom of the glass and instantly began to turn red.

Skunk looked down distractedly. Then, his eyes popped open. An unearthly scream pierced the air as the glass flew against the wagon and shattered into pieces. The jug hit the ground with a thud. Skunk scrambled off the wagon, his face awash with terror.

He was jabbering to himself, desperately trying to make sense of it all.

'But how? The curse? It can't be!'

Grabbing the water jug from the ground, he poured out the remaining liquid onto the grass, his frightened eyes darted back and forth between the clean water and the vampire trees in the distance.

Suddenly, he let loose a blood-curdling scream.

Across the creek, he saw the children, their hair and faces wet with blood. Against the raging water and the wind-whipped trees, they stood as erect and still as statues. Then, one by one they raised their hands, each pointing an accusing finger at Skunk. As they did, fresh blood began to flow from their hands, as if they too, had turned into wounded vampire trees.

'I never wanted you!' screamed Skunk, his face a deathly white. 'Ain't my idea! Ain't my idea!'

Scrambling back onto the wagon, he raised his whip against the startled mules. The wagon tore down the mountain, its back panel flapping in the wind. As it rounded the bend, the axe bounced off the wagon bed and onto the grass.

For what felt like eternity, Mount Armora held its breath.

Then, in the distance, the bird whistle sounded a triumphant note. Again and again.

22

The Hand of Fatima

Elven emerged from the bushes and made her way across the grass. In her excitement, her ankle no longer bothered her. Whooping and laughing, the children scrambled over the creek towards her, their previously expressionless faces now animated with joy.

The gamble had paid off. They had done it.

Ginger reached her first, her pale face still covered with red tree sap.

'Nice make-up, Ginger,' Elven said with a grin.

Ginger laughed and threw herself into Elven's arms. Her bright blue eyes overflowed with tears.

Not a moment later, they were surrounded by Matthew and the Mawoli kids who slapped Elven on the back and peppered her with a thousand questions. Out of the corner of her eye, Elven saw Ryan standing off to the side staring at them. Oh no, was he going to call her names like 'Eleven Elephant' or 'Darkie' again? She forced herself to turn and give him a wave.

'Hi, Elven,' Ryan said stiffly. 'Thank you.'

Elven nodded. 'You're welcome.'

'Look, I . . .' Ryan scratched his head. 'I'm sorry for all the unkind things I said to you.'

'That's okay,' she said, relieved.

Then, Coal ran over and shouted, 'Catch!'

Elven stretched out her hand as a plastic pouch sailed through the air, shattering into an explosion of red sap as it made contact with her palm.

The children burst out laughing.

'Now you're bloody like us!' one of the Mawoli kids shouted in glee.

'Sorry.' Coal stuck out his tongue. 'I had to save the last pouch for you.'

Elven laughed. She threw the pouch back at Coal but he dodged and the punctured bag landed next to Madam Green's feet.

'All right, all right,' Madam Green said, holding up her hands. 'Let's get back to the house now before anyone comes looking for you lot.'

'Will the miners come back?' Coal asked, his face suddenly solemn.

'I don't think so, but come along now. You'll be safe at my house.' Madam Green offered her arm to Elven, who took it gratefully.

The odd little group made their way across the clearing and was about to head up the trail when Ryan called out for them. Running over to the bushes, he picked up the axe that Skunk had used to cut the vampire tree.

'That might come in useful,' Madam Green said, giving Ryan a nod.

'Someone's drawn a creepy picture here,' Ryan said, examining the wooden handle. He held up the axe so they could all see the drawing of an open palm with an eye in the middle.

'Do you know what it means, Madam Green?' Ginger asked.

'I have no idea,' Madam Green said with a straight face.

But Elven knew she did. She had caught that barely perceptible twitch on Madam Green's cheek.

'Oh, I remember,' Coal exclaimed. 'It's the Hand of Fatima. Our old caretaker Mrs Bayou had a pendant painted with it. She used to wear it around her neck as protection against witches.'

'Witches?' exclaimed Ginger.

Ryan let out a whimper. 'On Mount Armora?'

A nervous murmur flitted through the group.

'I don't want to stay here if there are witches on the mountain,' whined the Mawoli girl called Anika. She clutched Ginger's arm with a nervous expression.

'Neither do I!' chimed in her brother, Ariki.

'Shush!' chided Ginger with a worried frown.

Elven shot Coal an accusing look but he only gave a nonchalant shrug. Next to her, she could feel Madam Green's arm tighten.

'Maybe it's safer in town,' suggested Ryan.

'Stuff and nonsense!' Elven cried, her voice fierce. 'There are no witches! And even if there were, why should you be afraid of them if you've done nothing wrong? Only wicked men like Skunk have cause for fear.'

She stared at the children for a good three seconds, daring them to challenge her statement. None did. Even Coal looked vaguely apologetic.

'Now,' she continued, 'unless you want to risk being caught, I suggest we hurry back to the house immediately.'

23

Hideout and Beyond

The children spent the following month with frayed nerves. Every time Gogo barked or a parrot screeched, someone would be convinced that the miners had discovered their hideout. However, with healthful meals and the fresh mountain air speeding up their recovery, the children's confidence began to grow. By late September, they were strong enough to help out with the various chores around the house.

The start of autumn proved surprisingly busy. A thunderstorm had caused damage to the house and shed roofs, both of which had to be rethatched. Madam Green's latest trip into Armora added new lodgers to the kennel—a poodle with an injured foot and two malnourished basset hounds. All three were initially fearful of humans, but under Gogo's no-nonsense guidance, they quickly adapted to life on the mountain.

Elven enjoyed the bustling atmosphere in the house, although there were times when she wished she had the attic room all to herself again. Now that she had become used to the silence of the mountain, it was hard to fall asleep amid the snoring, scratching, tossing, and turning of these other bodies next to her. When she eventually dozed off, she often woke in a panic, convinced that she was back in the crowded dormitory of the orphanage. At such times, she found herself searching under the faint moonlight for the mural on the wall. And when she spotted an animal or the girl with her head in the clouds, she would heave a sigh of relief because then, she would know she was safe.

But perhaps the hardest part to having so many people around was finding time to comb through Master Takuno's Sales Journal. Each of the fifty pages had twenty line items, which made for a staggering one thousand names to go through. Initially, Elven worked alone on the Puzzle Box in the wee hours of the morning before the household woke. But soon she realized having a friend beside her made the experience less lonely. As Coal was an early riser like her, she began recruiting his help. Even before the rooster sounded its first crow, they were already tiptoeing downstairs to pore over the Sales Journal.

Together, they eliminated about one-third of the surnames by striking out those with letters not found on her Puzzle Box. Of course, the list would have been even shorter if Master Takuno had also written down the first names of his clients. But given the circumstances, getting down to around two hundred entries in the first week was not a bad start.

After the first phase of elimination, Coal suggested that they go through another round of cuts. His rationale was this: The phrase YOU ARE MINE contained ten characters, out of which only E was repeated. Therefore, any name that had letters other than E repeated had to be eliminated. The exercise took them a good four days to complete and narrowed down their search to ten surnames: Aren, Enyou, Maneyo, Meyou, Muon, Neri, Noury, Ourinée, Ramin, and Reye.

'Seems like Master Takuno even had a few Mavarian clients,' Coal remarked as they read through the shortlist.

'How do you know?' Elven asked.

'Remember Mrs Bayou and her hog jerky? She once told me that names ending with "you" are usually Mavarian.'

'Interesting,' Elven said, impressed. 'Well, all we have to do now is arrange these last names on the box and then produce a corresponding first name with the remaining tiles.'

Coal nodded. 'Let's try Enyou and see what first names we can come up with.'

Elven shifted the tiles, trying different combinations of vowels and consonants until the name 'Marie Enyou' appeared.

'Darn,' Coal muttered as the Puzzle Box remained resolutely shut. 'What other names can you make from M, A, R, I, E?'

'Amire?'

'Never heard of it.'
'Raime?'
'Even worse.'
'All right, let's move on . . .'

After a week of trial and error, there were only five names that used up all ten of the letters: Marie Enyou, Arnie Meyou, May Ourinée, Amy Ourinée, and Maiee Noury.

The problem was, none of them opened the box.

Elven was at her wits' end. They had gone through a thousand names and still not uncovered the Key! Once again, she felt like the girl toiling in the kitchen in a bid to win the scholarship. All that effort and for what?

As the days grew shorter and the number of chores grew, she felt increasingly bothered—not just with the progress of the Puzzle Box but also with how life had changed since the children arrived. In the past, she could chat with Madam Green whenever and wherever she wanted. Now, an entire day would fly by without them sharing a joke or playing with Gogo. The days of picnicking by the river were but a distant memory. Madam Green was always tied up with something. If she wasn't tending to the garden, she was slaving away in the kitchen cooking large pots of food to feed them.

Elven wished she could take pride in how little Matthew and Ryan were coughing these days or how chatty the Mawoli siblings had become—certainly, a more generous spirit would. But she simply could not free herself of the melancholy weighing down her heart.

Then, there was the matter of the dwindling food supply. Following an exceptional pest outbreak that killed off the tomatoes, they were all sent to work harvesting the long beans and eggplants that had barely ripened in the garden. But it was clear that there wasn't enough to feed everyone for the month.

To Elven's guilty relief, the time had come for the inevitable conversation.

'I've been thinking . . .' Madam Green said, one evening at the end of supper. 'It's time we made a trip to the capital.'

'Why?' Ginger exclaimed, her blue eyes suddenly alert.

'Now that you're strong enough to travel, I need to let the authorities know what happened here,' Madam Green explained.

'Whatever for?' Matthew asked, clutching his cup of dandelion tea. 'We're safe here.'

Elven cleared her throat. 'It's not just about us,' she said. 'What if Morodon-Gore goes back to the orphanage and pulls the same trick on our friends? They could end up working in the mines around the country.'

The other children nodded reluctantly, but Matthew's frown dug deeper into his face. 'But it won't be so soon, right?' he asked. 'The scholarship's an annual thing. Morodon-Gore shouldn't return for nine months or so . . .'

'Nothing's for sure,' Madam Green said. 'It's hard to know the extent of this scheme. There could be other orphanages being targeted even as we speak. I wish

I could just report it to Armora's authorities, but I think this needs to go higher up. Straight to governor's office if possible.'

'Why would they believe us?' muttered Ryan.

'Why wouldn't they?' Madam Green asked. 'The governor is the most powerful official in the county. He'll be the best person to help all of you secure a future.'

'Wait!' Ginger shot up from her seat. 'You're sending us packing?'

Madam Green's smile faltered at the distressed expressions around the table. 'I wouldn't put it that way.' She reached out to give Ginger's hand a squeeze. 'But, as much as I love having you all around, I can't possibly keep you up on Mount Armora forever.'

'But I don't want to go into an orphanage,' complained Ryan. 'I like it here. What if they send us back to Hammond?'

His statement incited a round of protests. Even Ariki and Anika shook their heads and gritted their teeth. They had heard enough about the orphanage to know that it was not a place they would want to be.

'We have to return to the Southland,' they protested. 'Our parents may be imprisoned, but they're not dead!'

Elven cringed. Ever since Madam Green had brought up this topic with her, she'd had several sleepless nights thinking about how the others would react. Now, to her dismay, it was playing out the way she had imagined.

'Children, children!' Madam Green's voice sailed over the din. 'I have to find a permanent home for you. Somewhere safe so you can learn and grow. The mountain's no place for young ones like you and very soon, you'll be bored to tears at being stuck with a fuddy-duddy old woman.'

A peal of laughter rang across the kitchen.

'Besides, I don't have enough food to sustain all of us,' Madam Green added.

'You have tons of bananas . . .' Matthew said.

'Nobody can survive on bananas alone,' Madam Green replied gently. 'Now, Kenden's completely different. The governor's office has many good people, and they can make sure you have a proper education until you're sixteen—'

At this, the group turned sharply to Coal.

'So, you can do whatever you want?' Ginger asked him pointedly.

'Not *whatever*.' Coal's expression darkened. 'I have to find an apprenticeship in a kitchen. That is, if anyone will even take me without a reference letter.'

It's my fault that he hasn't got a reference, Elven thought. *If he hadn't helped me, he'd be apprenticing for someone now.*

'I bet Elven gets to stay here,' sulked Matthew.

'Does she?' asked Ginger, indignant.

'At least someone's worry-free,' Anika added, staring in Elven's direction.

Elven gulped down the water from her glass, unable to look Anika in the eye. What the others said was true but not completely.

'She can stay,' Madam Green admitted, exchanging a glance with Elven, 'if she chooses to.'

Elven stroked her eleventh finger uncertainly as she listened to the orphans complain about this thing and that. Going to Kenden with the others would mean going to school and being in the same city as Coal. In four years' time, she might even find employment in a top bakery in the capital. But doing that would mean leaving Madam Green, the dogs, the parrots, and Kraw the pigeon. Besides, what about Gogo? Hadn't Elven promised to look after him?

As always, it came down to the Puzzle Box. After months of pushing and pulling those darn tiles, Elven still hadn't made the tiniest bit of progress. She wondered if she ought to pursue another line of action. If she left for the capital, she could meet someone who might be able to point her in the right direction. If she stayed, she would be completely on her own.

'What do you want, Elven?' asked Ariki.

'I don't know,' Elven stuttered.

Matthew snorted while Ryan rolled his eyes.

'So, you're staying here while Coal leaves for the capital,' Anika said. 'I thought he's your best friend. Shouldn't you go along to help him? In Mawoli culture, best friends look out for each other.'

'I don't care about your stupid Mawoli culture!' Elven snapped. The words flew out of her mouth before she could stop herself. Anika and Ariki recoiled, and looked as if they had been slapped.

'Give her a break,' Coal said. 'She'll choose when the time comes.'

'Well, I wish I had *that* luxury,' Ginger muttered.

Elven clenched her jaw. 'Look here, all of you. I didn't say I'm not going to the capital. It's just that I haven't decided yet. I need to solve something first.

Once I'm ready, I'll clear out of here and happily readmit myself into an orphanage, all right?'

Out of the corner of her eye, Elven thought she saw Madam Green's mouth slacken. But when she turned to face the older woman, Madam Green merely nodded in encouragement.

'What's this thing you got to solve?' Matthew asked, interrupting her thoughts.

Elven bit her lips. She didn't feel like talking about the Puzzle Box but it didn't look like she had a choice. 'It's just something that may help me locate my father or family,' she said, shooting Coal a look. 'Something my mother left me.'

The answer seemed to satisfy the children's curiosity, and they went back to discussing their future, or the lack of it, in the capital.

'I suppose the only way to get all of us there is to take the train?' Coal asked.

The word 'train' elicited much excitement from the group, many of whom had never seen a real locomotive before. Even the Mawolis didn't mind delaying their return to the Southland in order to ride on one.

'But how can we afford the tickets?' Ryan asked.

Seven pairs of eyes focused on Madam Green who looked relieved at their about-turn.

'Why, we work for it of course!' Madam Green replied. 'This Saturday, Armora holds its annual Gold Festival. Since we've harvested a bumper crop of bananas, let's make a bake sale happen.'

Ginger scrambled to her feet. 'Let's get started, then.'

'Hold your horses!' Madam Green said, chuckling. 'Let's plan on finishing our chores first so we can devote the rest of the week to cooking and baking. The dogs need to be walked, and the birds need fresh fruit branches. Besides, we're going to have to get more flour and sugar if we want to do any serious baking.'

'I can go to Armora tomorrow,' Elven offered.

'Excellent! And while you're there, you might as well stock up on some grains for Kraw too.' Madam Green stood up, signalling the end of supper. 'Now, let's clear the table and get ready for bed. Anika and Ginger, it's your turn to do the dishes tonight.'

Chatting excitedly about the capital, the children brought their dishes to the sink. Elven skipped up to Coal, eager to share her latest discovery with him.

'I know where we went wrong—'

'Not now,' Coal cut in. 'I need to be alone, all right? To think.' Then, seeing her crestfallen face, he added in a low voice, 'We'll talk about your Puzzle Box in the morning, I promise.' Without waiting for her to answer, he turned and strode towards the door.

Elven stared as Coal disappeared into the frame of darkness. Until tonight, she had not realized the impact of her actions on him. Because of her wilful decision to look for Master Takuno, he had lost his future.

Best friends look out for each other. It didn't take a Mawoli to see how selfish she had been.

She had to be better than this. If Coal didn't have a reference letter, was there something else he could do? Could he 'make his own chance' as Mr Bora had once said?

An idea struck her.

Sprinting upstairs to the writing desk in the attic, she pulled out a piece of notepaper and started writing furiously.

'Dear Mr Bora,' she began. 'How would you like to meet my friend Coal? He's an excellent cook and a quick learner . . .'

24

Old Ties and Rivalries

The next morning felt like a drag with all the chores that had to be done before Elven could go into town. After lunch, she changed into a hand-me-down floral dress from Madam Green, which she hoped would make her seem more adult. It was maroon, with long puffy sleeves and layers of ruffles that reached her shins, since she was much shorter than its previous owner. After placing the Puzzle Box in her pocket, she secured the opening with a safety pin.

Outside, Madam Green had just finished inflating the bicycle tires. The Mawoli siblings appeared from the garden with a large, woven basket filled with fat, juicy lychees. Elven tensed up as they walked towards her. She had avoided them all morning because of what had happened the night before.

'What's the first rule of bartering?' Ariki asked as he attached the basket to the front of her bicycle. If he was still upset with her, he did not show it.

'Be polite?'

Anika let out a hysterical shriek, and even Madam Green couldn't resist a smile.

'Don't be mean, Anika,' Ariki chided. 'Orphanage kids have been protected all their lives.'

Protected? Me?

Anika made a face.

'The first rule,' Ariki said, ignoring his sister, 'is never make the first offer.'

'Ask the store manager what he's willing to give you,' Anika said, 'then bargain for more.'

'But what if he refuses?' Elven asked.

'Then, at least you tried,' Anika said, her hands squarely on her hips.

'Wait.' Madam Green disappeared into the house and returned with a small sack. 'Why don't you throw in a few eggplants? These are getting overripe anyway.'

'But don't show him the eggplants until he refuses your counter offer!' Ariki added with a cunning smile.

'Are you sure you don't want to come along?' Elven asked them as she secured her headscarf. 'You're so much better at this than I am.'

The siblings chuckled.

'No, thanks,' Ariki said. 'We're heading into the forest with the others. The parrots need more fruit branches.'

'Birds are much better company than the Armorians,' Anika quipped. 'See you back at the aviary!'

As Elven turned to go, Madam Green took her hand and slipped her two cents. 'Get yourself a treat,' she whispered.

With the produce in the basket, Elven hitched up her dress and headed down the mountain. But, as she soon discovered, the brakes had become so stiff that she had to resort to using her legs to slow the bike down. As she cycled past the Heritage Museum, she made a note to call on Mr Long on her way home. Maybe he would have something interesting to say about anagrams.

The general store was about fifteen minutes away from the plaza. Outside the white clapboard building, a group of restless men was gathered on the sidewalk smoking and talking loudly. Elven lowered her head as she passed them, parking her bicycle in a spot visible from the entrance. After hesitating slightly, she detached her basket of produce and strode inside.

Two elderly women standing by the fruit bin glanced at her briefly before resuming their conversation. To the left of the door, a man with thinning hair was reading the papers next to the cash register.

'Good afternoon!' Elven said, putting her basket on the counter. 'I'm here to trade some lychees for flour and sugar.'

The store manager lifted the basket lid, poked around with his fingers, and held up a lychee to the light. 'Not bad,' he said after a thorough examination. 'How much do you want for them?'

'How much would you give for them?' Elven asked, remembering Ariki's words.

The store manager looked a little surprised, but he answered, 'Would you take two bags of flour and a bag of sugar?'

'Three bags of flour and two bags of sugar.'

'Three bags of flour *or* two bags of sugar.'

'Three bags of flour and two bags of sugar, and I'll throw in these delicious eggplants.'

The store manager picked up the eggplants and examined them. 'They look too ripe,' he grumbled. 'Three bags of flour and one bag of sugar.'

'Deal!' Elven said, reaching out to shake the manager's hand.

'Let me attend to these ladies here first and I'll get your goods out.'

Giddy with success, Elven wandered between the shelves while the manager served the other customers. This was her first time inside a store and the variety of foodstuff surprised her. After a while, her eyes settled on the ice cream counter.

'How much for an ice cream cone?' she asked when the store manager was done.

'Five cents.'

'I only have two,' Elven said, her heart sinking. 'What can I buy?'

'Not much. I suppose I can sell you a slice of buko pie, but I'll have to scoop out the filling. Or you can buy a cupcake without the icing.'

For a moment, Elven thought he was joking. But the man's unsmiling demeanour suggested anything but.

'How about if I get the ice cream without the cone?'

The store manager scratched his chin. 'I suppose I could serve it to you in a dish,' he said. 'But you'll have to eat it here because I can't afford people running away with my dish and spoon.'

'Of course.' Elven handed over her money quickly, afraid he would change his mind. 'Vanilla, please.' She hopped onto the bar stool and swung her legs back and forth as the store manager scooped up the ice cream and placed it in front of her.

Elven swallowed a spoonful of the ice cream and felt it slide down her throat. It was sweet, cold, and smooth; better than she had imagined.

'Oh, my goodness!' she cried out. 'This is the best thing I've ever eaten!'

'I agree,' a familiar voice said. 'Another scoop of ice cream for the young lady, please.'

Elven turned and gave a shriek of delight when she saw Mr Long standing behind her.

'Ah, Mr Long,' said the store manager, adding more ice cream to the dish. 'We hardly ever see you at our town hall meetings.'

'It's a new game these days, one for the young people. I'm just happy to preserve the old.' Mr Long removed his hat and sat down next to Elven. 'Any luck with your Puzzle Box?' he asked, smiling at her.

'I didn't think you'd remember me,' Elven said shyly.

'I don't get many girls coming in with Puzzle Boxes,' Mr Long replied, his eyes twinkling. 'So, did you find Master Takuno?'

Elven shook her head. She recounted her trip to Bowler Hat Lake, the news of Master Takuno's death, and how the Fossil Fair had yielded the most elusive of clues. 'If it's true—what Abe said—then I should be able to open the Puzzle Box if I know the right anagram.'

'I should have known.' Mr Long chuckled to himself. 'Now you understand why he carved an acorn on his seal, under the symbol of Mount Armora?'

'Because there are acorns buried under Mount Armora?'

'An acorn is also known as an oak nut,' Mr Long said. 'What do you get when you rearrange "oak nut"?'

'Oh!' Elven exclaimed. 'Takuno!'

They burst into laughter.

'I'm almost certain that my Key is a name,' Elven said. She debated whether to reveal the fact that she had gotten hold of Master Takuno's Sales Journal but decided to keep it a secret, lest Mr Long should think badly of her.

'And what names have you got?'

'None that work,' Elven replied. She brought out the box from her pocket and handed it to him.

'AMY OURINEE . . .' Mr Long rubbed his thumb across the two missing tiles in the bottom row after AMY. 'I used to know a most spirited little girl by that name, except that her mother spelled it the traditional Cantorean way. Oh yes, I remember her well.' He fell silent for a while before returning his gaze to the box. 'Hmm, I suspect you have a five-letter word in there.'

'Why do you say so?'

'You have five tiles across the lid of the box.'

'And?'

'And Master Takuno was a precise man.'

Elven thought for a bit and said, 'Well, the last name "Meyou" has five letters.'

'Let's give it a try.' Mr Long pushed the tiles about until the words IRENA MEYOU appeared.

'Irena!' Elven leaned in for a closer look. She had no idea that the ARNIE MEYOU she had come up with earlier could be rearranged into a female name.

'Irena's a very common name in these parts,' Mr Long said, exerting pressure on the box.

Elven's heart skipped a beat. Could this be it?

The box stared back at them, defiant.

'Ah well.' Mr Long placed the money on the counter and patted Elven on the shoulder. 'Do come by when you want someone to talk to. There's nothing in this world that can't be solved. Not even a Key.'

Elven pursed her lips. 'But if you can't solve it, who can?'

Mr Long's right hand froze above the hat on the counter. 'If there's anyone in this world who can open your box, it'll be the mayor.' Mr Long's eyes glazed over, as if obscured by some unpleasant memory. 'You see, he was Takuno's apprentice—his only apprentice.'

'That's why he wanted to buy the workshop!' Elven exclaimed before realizing her slip of tongue.

'Oh, you've heard,' Mr Long said absent-mindedly as he put on his hat. 'News travels fast, I suppose. But still, I can't imagine why he, of all people, would want to acquire Takuno's place.'

'Because he's a sentimental man?' Elven asked, recalling the mayor's words.

'Sentimental?' Mr Long gave a cynical smile. 'Mayor Moore's as sentimental as an automaton. Did you know that he and Master Takuno fell out years ago?' The smile faded and a look of pain flitted across Mr Long's deeply lined face. 'In fact, he was the reason why Master Takuno moved away.'

'What do you mean?'

'Before he became mayor, Moore built a factory to manufacture Puzzle Boxes about five miles from here,' Mr Long replied. 'Master Takuno just couldn't compete. For the cost of a handcrafted box, you could buy ten factory-made ones. And the young people, they fall in and out of love so easily these days. How many love stories last forever? How many of them warrant spending over a hundred dollars on a Takuno box? Though these machine-made boxes are inferior in quality, they're good enough for the durations of these short affairs. And that's what most people want: good enough.'

Elven felt a sudden chill as Abe's words came back to her—or was it too much ice cream? Abe had said that Master Takuno died of a heart attack. Could the real cause be a broken heart?

'Why did he drive Master Takuno out of business?' Elven asked.

'Money, I suppose. And ambition.' Mr Long shook his head disapprovingly. 'He was ruthless, and he knew he would never be as good as Master Takuno. But the mayor was as talented and intelligent as they came. If he couldn't surpass Master Takuno in skill, he would win by sheer volume and cost . . . Poor Takuno, he wouldn't compromise on his workmanship. But, in the end, he had to admit defeat.'

The rest of Mr Long's words were lost on Elven. At some point, she had the vague impression of saying goodbye to him. As she sat staring at the ice cream dish, all Elven could think of was how she might have to beg the mayor for help one day. The idea filled her with dread.

'Here you go!' The store manager placed her basket on the counter with a thump. He had emptied the lychees and replaced them with bags of flour and sugar.

'Thank you, sir.' Elven tucked the Puzzle Box into her pocket quickly.

'You be careful on your way home.' The store manager pointed to a poster on the wall next to them. Under the words 'MISSING' was a picture of a girl about Elven's age. She had dark eyes and shoulder-length brown hair, not unlike hers. 'A thirteen-year-old girl went missing a few days ago in broad daylight. The chief hasn't found her yet but everyone knows who did it.'

'Who?'

The store manager leaned over the counter and whispered conspiratorially, 'The witch, of course.'

25

The Evil Mountain Witch

Seeing the surprise on Elven's face, the store manager added, 'You must know of the witch who lives up in the mountain.'

'But it's just a story,' Elven said.

The store manager gave a harrumph. 'Have you been up the mountain after dusk?' Before Elven could reply, he leaned across the counter and hissed, 'Well I have, and to this day I get the shivers just thinking about that fateful night.'

Elven wanted to correct him, but thought better of it. The strange look on his face disturbed her. She tightened her headscarf and slipped off the stool.

'I still remember that cold spring day as if it were yesterday,' the store manager carried on, with no intention of leaving her alone. 'I was up the mountain hunting rabbits. So engrossed was I that I went off the trail and lost track of time. Before I knew it, the sun had set. After wandering around in panic, I spied a warm orange glow in the distance. As I got closer, I was glad to see that it was a nice-looking house with window shutters. I made my way towards it, praying hard that a kind soul would shelter me for the night. But in my haste, I tripped and fell across a log.

'Suddenly the air was filled with the screeches and screams of children. "I'm hungry!" cried one. "Water, water!" cried another. "Feed me!" I picked myself up and was about to investigate further when the wolves started howling. The door of the house flung open and a grotesque silhouette appeared in the doorway. I could not see her face for the light was behind her, thank goodness, but it was clear that she was a witch.

'Screeching in anger, she raised her broom to cast a spell on me. In defence, I drew my bow. I am a good marksman and my arrows do not miss. What I didn't expect was that upon striking her, it bounced off her chest like a ball off the wall. The witch recoiled in surprise but did not fall. The children screeched angrily, mocking my stupidity. I ran as fast as my feet would carry me. By God's grace, I stumbled upon a creek and following it downhill, I was able to find my way back.'

'Are you sure that was a witch?' Elven asked. The description of the house sounded suspiciously like Madam Green's cottage.

'Of course!' Sweat had formed on the store manager's red excited face. Even his scalp appeared shiny beneath his combed-back hair. 'God knows what'd have happened if I'd not gotten away quickly.' He pulled out a handkerchief from his pocket and gave his face a good wipe. 'To this day, I make it my civic duty to warn any foolhardy travellers from venturing up the mountain.'

'But couldn't it have been a misunderstanding? I mean, you could have heard—'

The store manager thumped the counter with his fist, making Elven jump. 'There was no mistake! Are you saying that I'm a liar? Or that the other townsfolk who saw her are liars?'

'No, sir, I didn't mean that—'

'She gave me the evil eye once,' interrupted someone.

Elven turned and saw that it was a pale-looking woman with a stoop. A crowd had gathered around, eager to hear more. 'I was taken ill a week later and have never quite recovered. Those green eyes . . . they haunt my dreams.'

'My brave boy Sammy saw the witch in our plaza,' one of the customers chimed in. 'Skulking around in her witchy, black headscarf, thinking we wouldn't recognize her.'

An alarm went off in Elven's head.

'I've seen her too at night,' said another woman. 'Stealing our dogs, she was.'

'Wait, do you mean the *unwanted* dogs?' Elven asked. Her pulse quickened. Surely they were not talking about Madam Green? How could they think that she was a witch for saving their abandoned pets?

'Wanted or unwanted, what does it matter?' the store manager sneered.

'But what does she want with them?' asked a wide-eyed girl in a trembling voice.

'Unspeakable horrors.' The store manager shakes his head grimly at the crowd. 'Maybe she eats them, maybe she turns them into beasts. How else would you explain the large pack of wolves I saw? Mark my word, there are unnatural things happening up on the mountain.'

'Why do we allow this foul creature to wander about town casting spells and kidnapping innocent children?' grumbled a surly man. 'Surely the chief must do something about it.'

Elven was about to protest but her words were drowned out by a woman's loud voice.

'But he won't! I've talked to him and he won't!' the woman cried. 'Says we haven't got proof.'

'The chief's got a point,' an old man wheezed. 'This is pure speculation.'

'And a wild one as such,' muttered the old woman by his side.

'Have you two forgotten Ah Ming?' The store manager cast a disgusted look at the dissenters. 'My little brother took to his deathbed within a week of my encounter with the witch. Do you truly believe this is a coincidence?'

'Ah Ming and the missing girl are proof enough!' a burly man in dungarees shouted, his eyes flashing with anger.

'Must we wait before a second child disappears?' cried a mother, rocking her baby. 'Before *my* baby disappears?'

'Folks, folks!' The store manager raised his hands in a bid to silence the squabbling. 'We Armorians are peace-loving people. We abide by the law, we pay our taxes, we keep our streets clean. But this is not a time of peace. And the supernatural follows none of Man's laws. We have waited long enough for the chief to protect us. And he has let us down! It is up to us to cast evil out of our beloved Mount Armora! For every minute we delay, the witch grows stronger on the blood of her half-Mawoli slaves!'

'Aye, aye!' muttered several people.

'It is time we take things into our own hands,' a young man said. His friends murmured in approval.

'You're jumping to conclusions!' Elven shouted. 'She's not a witch!'

'What do *you* know?' The group glared at her, challenging her to say more. These were hard men, like Skunk. Men who knew no boundaries. Men who knew no fear.

Still, if she did not speak up for Madam Green, who would? Heart pounding, she went on, 'The woman who lives on Mount Armora is an ordinary person. Except that she has done extraordinary things that you're not even aware of. Do you know that abandoned gold mine? She has just saved it—'

'That's right!' the store manager cut in. 'The witch's house is off the mountain trail, not far from where the gold mine meets the creek.'

An excited murmur spread through the crowd.

'It's now or never!' yelled the man in the dungarees. 'Today, we shall be heroes and rid Armora of a great evil!'

To Elven's dismay, the townsfolk nodded in agreement, their once-friendly eyes now glistening with danger.

Oh God, what have I done? Hugging the heavy basket tight to her, Elven made straight for the open door. Around her, the feverish crowd was spreading out, slithering down the alleys and streets like venomous snakes on the prowl.

'Please God,' Elven whispered as she steered her bicycle through the crowd, 'Help me get there before it's too late.'

26

The Purveyor of Dreams

The ride up the mountain felt like it would never end. Just when her legs were about to give out, the house came into sight. Elven jumped off her bicycle and ran up the garden path.

'Madam Green!' she shouted, flinging open the wooden door so hard that it thumped against the wall.

There was a loud crash as something hit the floor.

Elven skidded to a stop. Madam Green was standing on a chair next to the kitchen armoire, staring at her in shock. On the floor was a pile of letters that had spilled out of a large red box.

'I . . . I was just putting some . . . old things away,' Madam Green said, sounding flustered. 'Why don't you run along and find the others in the aviary?'

'Let me help you.' Elven pulled off her headscarf and picked up the box. It looked oddly familiar. Had she seen it before somewhere?

Examining the rusty red paint, the answer came to her in a flash. Why, of course! It was back when she first arrived at the house. Hadn't she seen Madam Green crying while hunched over that red box?

'It's fine, really.' Madam Green got down from the chair and took the box from her. 'I can manage on my own.' Working quickly, she scooped the fallen letters into the box, like she was afraid that Elven would ask about them.

As Elven looked around her, an old photograph caught her eye. She picked it up and held it up to the window. In it, a wavy-haired woman and a small girl stood next to a metal cage, their hair brilliant in the bright sunshine. The cage was tall, much taller than the young woman, and its narrow bars were cast into the concrete floor. A large peacock preened in the corner of the cage, his half-missing plumage spread out like a broken fan. The woman, unlike the girl, was not enthralled. She had turned her face to the photographer and was saying something. Her eyebrows were knitted in sadness.

'Give that to me!' Madam Green shouted, snatching the photograph from her so violently that Elven feared she might have torn it apart.

'Don't!' Elven's forearm went up to her face automatically, shielding her face against a potential attack. Visions of Mrs Monteiro's cane flashed before her. Staggering away from the table, Elven tripped against the chair, which fell with a crash.

'I'm so sorry.' Madam Green's voice was wrung with agony. 'I'm so sorry I frightened you. I would *never* hit you. Never.'

Elven let down her arm slowly.

Madam Green crouched down next to her, her face tense with regret. She smoothed out the crumpled corner of the photograph and handed it over to Elven. 'Her name is Aimee,' she said softly. 'This is the last photograph I have of us. Well, I didn't know that back then, of course.'

Elven stared at the girl, who looked about six or seven. 'She's your daughter?'

Madam Green nodded.

'Twenty-three years ago,' she said, 'I had a husband and a daughter. We lived in the finest house in Armora, ate the finest food, and dressed in the most expensive clothes. But it wasn't just us. At that time, Armora was in the middle of a gold rush. From being poor all their lives, the citizens were suddenly able to acquire anything they wished. Clothes, jewels, imported wine; it was an age of excesses. My husband was a successful businessman—"a purveyor of dreams" as he often called himself.'

'What's a purveyor?' Elven asked.

'A purveyor provides what is demanded. But Talford did not bring in mundane things like cheese, or bicycles, or paintings. He imported dreams; any dream, the wilder the better, for he could charge so much more for them. If someone wanted caviar from France, Talford would bring it in. If they wanted a coat made from a Siberian fox, Talford would have it made. There was nothing you couldn't get at his emporium.

'It was at that time when the town's love affair with pets started. In the short course of five years, a menagerie of animals trotted through Armora. People started out with common ones like dogs, cats, and goldfish, but when they grew tired of them, my husband started importing more and more exotic animals. Snakes, monkeys, sugar gliders—'

'Parrots?'

'Yes, and parrots.'

'But where did people keep the animals they didn't want?' Elven asked, even though she had a sinking feeling about what the answer was.

'You're quick, Elven . . . quicker than I was,' Madam Green said in a weak voice. 'When the Armorians got bored of their pets—even the exotic ones—they traded them in for new ones. The abandoned pets were sent up Mount Armora to a shelter. Or at least that's what I thought.

'The day we took that photograph was the day I uncovered the truth. You see, I had badgered Talford to take us to this "shelter". I'd imagined it to be a happy place. A peaceable kingdom. Only it was no shelter. The animals were packed in horrendous, crowded cages so small that some could no longer walk properly, and then killed for what they could provide. The snakes and crocodiles were skinned for their leather. The peacock in the photograph had his feathers plucked for hats. Dogs and ponies were slaughtered for their meat.

'It was a torture farm. A slaughterhouse! When I realized the truth, I knew I had to do something. But who could I go to? There was nothing illegal about what Talford was doing. So, I did the only thing I could do. I set fire to the shelter. But the strange thing was, Talford wasn't furious at me, not for long anyway. Shortly after he confronted me, he began acting as if the whole thing had just been an accident. Even though we both knew otherwise.'

Madam Green struggled to keep her voice even. 'Then, a month later, Talford suggested that I take a trip to visit my mother. I was exhausted by the whole chain of events and so I did, leaving Aimee with him and the nanny. When I came back, the house was empty. They were gone, along with all the other servants. I made calls to the police chief, even the governor who had once been a customer of ours. I spoke to every single Armorian I knew, but no one could tell me where they were. Talford had taken the one person that mattered most to me.'

'But someone must have known!' Elven cried. 'They couldn't have just vanished into thin air.'

'Nobody knew,' Madam Green's voice dipped to a whisper, 'or if they did, they pretended not to. I never saw Aimee again.' She blinked, forcing back her tears. 'Thinking back, it was not surprising for Talford to pack up. He knew that the mining was coming to an end. Without its wealth, Armora could no longer sustain his business. Shortly after they left, the accusations started. Aimee's disappearance became *my* doing. Parents forbade their children from talking to me and my house got vandalized. Not long after, I received death threats. For my own safety, I had no choice but to move up the mountain.'

'Is that why you only ever go into Armora after dark? And always wearing your headscarf so no one recognizes you?'

Madam Green nodded. 'They call me the mountain witch. If there is a drought, it's because of me. If a man falls ill and dies, it's because of a spell I had cast. If a child behaves badly then it is I who had enchanted her.'

'That's not fair! You didn't know Talford was going to take your daughter away.'

'No, I didn't, but it doesn't matter any more.' Madam Green reached out and gently removed the photograph from Elven's tightly clenched hands. 'Aimee's gone. Perhaps she's even forgotten me. Life has moved on and so must I. It's like riding a bicycle, you see. One can only pedal forward, not backward.'

'But you need to tell them the truth.' Elven clutched Madam Green's arm. 'A girl has gone missing and they think you kidnapped her. They're coming to get you!'

'Well, let them come,' Madam Green said in a hard voice. 'They won't find her here.' She replaced the photograph inside the box and pressed the lid close. 'Besides, it doesn't matter what I say.'

'They're going to destroy this place!' Elven shouted. How could Madam Green be so stubborn? 'Don't you care about our home?'

Suddenly, they heard yells and the loud barking of Gogo from outside the house. The deafening crack of a rifle cut through the air. Then, all was unbearably silent.

27

The Mob

'Gogo!' Elven cried, jumping to her feet.

'Stop!' Madam Green shouted, grabbing Elven's arm. 'Stay here.'

Elven opened her mouth to protest but the look on Madam Green's face was enough to make her close it right back.

'Stay hidden,' Madam Green instructed as she ventured out of the door. Elven crawled over to the window, anxious to know what had happened to Gogo but frightened of what she would see.

'Can I help you gentlemen?' she heard Madam Green's voice ring out.

Elven peeked out from behind the curtains and immediately, a gasp escaped from her lips. A small army of men had arrived on horses and wagons. Armed with rifles and ropes, they dismounted and approached the house, their faces pinched like Rottweilers ready to pounce. A large man with wild hair and stubble stepped forward and spat on the ground.

'Where is she, witch?' he snarled.

'That's no way to address a lady,' Madam Green replied in an even tone. 'I have no idea what you're talking about.'

'Hand over the missing girl!'

'I do not have a missing girl here. Sir, I have to ask you to leave imme—'

Her words were interrupted by excited shouts. 'Good Lord! The store manager was right!'

The crowd parted and to Elven's horror, a couple of young men shoved Coal and the children into the middle.

'Look what I found in the big cage behind, Ojas!' one of them said to the man. 'Those stories are true! Young children taken as slaves and worked to their bones—'

'Oh, I'm glad someone's learned the truth!' interrupted Ryan. 'I never want to work in a mine again.'

Elven's body turned to jelly. *Ryan! You and your big mouth! Now they think Madam Green imprisoned you here!*

Ojas' crooked nose quivered in disgust. 'Ah, that's what you do up here, witch! Sending children to dig up gold for you! Is that what strengthens your black magic?'

'Stuff and nonsense!' Madam Green's voice took on a hard edge. 'I ask you for the last time to leave my property right now!'

'Or what?' Ojas jeered. He raised his hands like a conjurer. 'Salt!'

The mob reached into their pockets and without warning, a shower of white crystals pelted down on Madam Green. The children yelped and covered their faces but Madam Green stood unflinching until the last fistful of salt hit the ground. Then, she reached up and shook her shawl with a cold laugh.

'What's this?' she asked in a bemused voice. 'An a-salt?'

The children broke out in giggles but they were immediately cut off by Ojas.

'She's powerless now!' he shouted. 'Tie her up!'

Elven could bear it no longer. If Madam Green was going to give her a hard time, so be it! She leaped up from behind the window and burst through the doorway.

'Stop!' Elven cried, her hands raised above her head. 'It's all a misunderstanding!'

Ojas stepped back, startled. But a second later, he yelled out, 'The missing girl! We've found the missing girl!'

A triumphant cheer rang out among the mob.

'Don't be afraid, child.' A foul-smelling woman with a missing front tooth rushed forward to embrace Elven. 'We're bringing you home.'

'I'm not the missing girl! You've made a mistake!' Elven protested, pushing her away. 'Those are children we saved from the miners!'

But her cries were drowned out by the shouts of the mob. A large man swung Elven up over his shoulders and started across the garden. As she struggled to get free, Elven saw that several others had cornered Madam Green.

Suddenly, the man let out a loud scream. Still holding onto Elven, he tumbled sideways and hit the ground hard. Elven rolled away, stunned and confused, before she realized what had happened. Wrapped around his leg was dear old Gogo, clinging on for dear life as the man flailed about, trying to kick him off.

'Good dog!' Elven scrambled off the vegetable patch, searching for Madam Green. But she was nowhere to be seen. Instead, she found the shed engulfed in flames and billowing smoke.

'No, no, no! Not the harvest!' she cried.

'We've got to put out the fire!' shouted Coal from behind the burning shed. Somehow, he had escaped the mob and was beating the flames with a hemp sack. Ignoring Coal's warning, Elven ran into the shed, hoping to rescue as much of the dried goods as possible. But the smoke stung her eyes and pressed down on her like a heavy blanket. In the end, she barely made it out with a sack of rice. As Elven lay coughing on the ground, she heard Gogo's heart-wrenching yelps in the distance. Through her tears, she saw him thrashing about under a weighted net.

'Let him go, you monsters!' It was Madam Green. Her hair was in disarray and her left shoulder was showing through her ripped sleeve.

'Don't move,' shouted one of the men from the general store—the one in the dungarees, 'or I'll put a bullet through you.' He lifted his rifle and pointed it right at her.

Madam Green ignored him and sprinted towards Gogo. But before she could take more than a few steps, the man in dungarees had swung his rifle butt at her face. Madam Green let out a scream and collapsed to the ground. Two men ran forward, one grabbing her by the shoulders and the other twisting her arms behind her back. As Madam Green struggled to get free, blood poured from the corner of her mouth, staining her shirt red.

Elven's heart broke into a million pieces. She had never seen Madam Green so helpless, so humiliated before. She was about to cry out when Coal put his hand over her mouth and pulled her behind the bushes.

'We're outnumbered,' he hissed, pushing her back on the grass.

'We can find the others!'

'It's too late.' He pointed towards the house and she saw that he was right. The other children were being herded into a wagon, their hands tied behind their backs. When Anika tried to make a desperate attempt to escape, one of the men gave her such a hard slap that she fell to the ground. Within moments, she was shoved into the wagon and the back panel slammed shut. Elven and Coal watched helplessly as a man put a sack over Madam Green's head and dragged her into another wagon. Amid the triumphant chants, Ojas shouted a command and the horses tore down the mountain at a demonic speed.

28

Friends in High Places

Elven stared at the smouldering pile of timber that had once held their harvest. Next to it, the vegetable garden was in shambles. The rows of newly planted seedlings had been trampled on and even the bamboo trellis for the long beans had collapsed into a pile. In the distance was a bundle of orange on the charred ground.

No, not the parrots.

She twisted her head away and threw up. Their secret house in the mountain, once a safe haven, was now a broken fortress. And it was all her fault. If she hadn't mentioned the abandoned mine, the mob wouldn't have figured out Madam Green's location. Now, anyone could walk in on them anytime and take anything they wanted.

'What do we do now?' Coal asked, coming up to her. His face was black with soot and a wet, open wound glistened on his right arm, where he must have fallen.

For once, she had no answer. All she had worked for was gone. Even the only person who cared about her could be dead by now. What was the point of trying so hard if everything was just going to be destroyed in the blink of an eye? Maybe if she had never left the orphanage, none of this would have happened. This was the universe's way of punishing her for wanting more than what she deserved. Why did she need to open the Puzzle Box? Why couldn't she have accepted the fact that love didn't come to people like her? She should have stayed quiet, invisible, content with her lot in life . . .

'It's not too late to return to the orphanage,' Elven muttered.

'What are you talking about?' Coal snapped.

'Us charging into town will only make things worse.' Tears welled up in her eyes as she thought of how she had defied Madam Green's instructions to stay hidden. 'It's two of us against hundreds of locals. What can we do?'

'You can talk to people. Find help!'

'Who would believe the words of a half-breed?' Elven unfastened the safety pin holding her pocket together and removed the Puzzle Box. 'Hammond may still take us in and we can continue working on the Puzzle—'

'To hell with this stupid box,' Coal cursed, slapping it out of her hand. Elven shrieked as her beloved box flew and landed on the ground with a thud. 'I'm sick of this self-pity!' Coal shouted. 'This selfishness! You're so focused on solving your Puzzle Box that you've lost sight of what you have. Elven, do you think the Puzzle Box can give you more than what Madam Green has given you? Given *us*? Is this how you repay her? Why not harness a fifth of the ingenuity and grit you've spent chasing after the answer on saving her?'

A soft bark interrupted his words.

'Gogo?' Elven cried, running towards the direction of the barks. Beneath a collapsed fence, she spotted Gogo's paws entangled in the net that trapped him. Together with Coal's help, she pushed away the obstruction and freed Gogo.

'Here's a half-breed who wouldn't give up,' Coal said in a quiet voice.

Elven glanced back at the Puzzle Box and then at Gogo and Coal. Why had she thought that this inanimate object would solve her life's problems? It felt laughable to think that she had actually believed a genie would pop out of it and make her wishes come true.

'You're right,' she said at last. 'Half-breeds don't give up.'

'There must be somebody who knows Madam Green. Somebody who can stop this madness.'

Elven jumped up. 'Mr Bora! We have to send the pigeon to him. He knows many important people in Kenden. One of them may be able to help.'

Coal's eyes narrowed. 'Kenden's at least half an hour away by horse. Do we wait here, then?'

'No,' said Elven, picking up the Puzzle Box. 'We go see my friend.'

* * *

It was late afternoon by the time they arrived at Harris' house. Elven stood under the raintree next to the pavement and stared at the magnificent mansion across the lawn. Taking a deep breath, she was about to shout

out Harris' name when Gogo began barking furiously at the tree.

'What's wrong?' No sooner had the words left Elven's mouth than a long, brown creature dropped onto her shoulder from the tree branch above, causing her to spring away in horror. 'Snake!' she cried, knocking into Coal, her arms flailing.

Laughter broke out above her. 'Don't you recognize a rope when you see one?'

There, hidden among the branches, was Harris peering down at her from a plank of wood. No, not a plank of wood. A tree house!

Elven was about to reply when a woman's shrill voice rang out from the mansion.

'Master Harris, are you all right?'

'I'm fine! Saw a rat, that's all!' Harris shouted back. He gave Coal a wave and shook the knotted rope at them with a grin. 'Come on up before the governess sees you.'

The threat of being caught was enough to send Elven scrambling up the knotted rope. Luckily, the tree house was only six or seven feet above ground. Coal hooked Gogo's leash to the fence and tried to pull himself up the rope. But his bad leg gave him a lot of trouble and he couldn't get a firm grip. Finally, with Elven and Harris pulling the rope up, he made it to the top of the smooth timber platform.

'Are you here to watch the witch trial?' Harris asked, panting. He was dressed much more casually today in a white shirt and brown trousers held up by a pair of suspenders.

Elven and Coal exchanged a stricken look.

'Look,' Elven said. 'I know you've believed in the evil mountain witch all your life. But she's not real. She's simply a fictitious character adults made up to scare you into doing what they want.'

'Or worse,' added Coal, 'a convenient scapegoat to shoulder the blame whenever something bad happens.'

As they told him about the mob that had stormed the mountain, Harris' face grew pale. 'If what you say is true,' he said, 'we're running out of time. They will burn her if they find her guilty of witchcraft.'

Coal's mouth fell open. 'How can we stop them? We don't even know where the missing girl is.'

Harris looked at Elven with a strange expression. 'Didn't you say they thought you were the missing girl?' When she nodded, he continued, 'What if you told them who you really are?'

Elven frowned. 'But I'm a nobody . . .' Did Harris want her to announce to the whole world that she was a runaway? What if Hammond caught wind of her whereabouts?

Harris slapped his forehead in exasperation. 'I mean, if they insist Madam Green kidnapped you—the missing girl—and you prove you aren't the missing girl, wouldn't their whole testimony fall flat?'

'Wait,' Elven said. 'Do you know who the missing girl's parents are? If we can convince them to come with us then we can prove without a doubt that Ojas is wrong.'

'That's a brilliant idea!' Harris grabbed the rope and swung himself off the platform. 'I know where the Razzaks live. Follow me.'

* * *

'I recognize this place,' Coal said, his face darkening.

It turned out that the Razzaks owned the inn next to the stable—the one in which the children had been held prisoners. A niggling thought clawed at Elven as they made their way across the street to the small apartment at the back of the building. On the night that she had eavesdropped on the innkeeper's conversation with his wife, Mrs Razzak had warned her husband not to offend someone called Gordon. Could their daughter's disappearance have something to do with this mysterious person?

Harris knocked on the door and a moment later, it swung open to reveal the harried figure of Mrs Razzak in a navy blue dress.

'This is not a good time, children,' she grumbled as she put on her hat. 'I'm about to go out. They've found my daughter in the witch's cottage.'

'Actually they haven't,' Elven said, stepping forward with Gogo. 'They insist I'm your daughter, and they've captured an innocent woman based on this fraudulent claim.'

'No, no, it can't be true,' Mrs Razzak insisted. 'Everyone tells me Ojas has found her.'

'Nobody has seen her, and Ojas doesn't care about your daughter,' Harris said. 'Do you really trust a man who gets into a brawl every other week?'

Mrs Razzak's face fell.

'Please, you have to help clear Madam Green's name,' Elven pleaded. 'If you've grown up in this town, you'll remember the emporium. Madam Green was the owner's wife and she lived in Armora for many years before vicious gossip drove her up the mountain.'

'The emporium . . .' A look of nostalgia came over Mrs Razzak's face. 'Why yes, as a child, my Papa used to bring me there. It was a wonderful place stocked with toys and confectionery, and pets! I always spent my birthdays in the emporium and a beautiful lady with green eyes would give me free lollipops—'

'That's her! That's Madam Green.' Elven was suddenly filled with hope. If someone like Mrs Razzak could remember Madam Green's kindness then there would be others. Others they could convince.

'Nina, who are you talking to?' came a man's gruff voice from inside the apartment.

'We have to help these children, dear,' Mrs Razzak shouted back. 'Ojas has gone off his rocker and is about to burn an innocent woman alive.'

The sound of heavy footsteps echoed down the dim hallway as Mrs Razzak turned sideways to greet the speaker. A short, wiry man stepped into the light, his face scrunched up in a scowl.

'What's that got to do with—' He froze, mouth agape, eyes bulging as he gawked at Coal and Elven. 'You . . . you two . . .'

Elven stared back, confused. Mr Razzak's face was oddly familiar but it couldn't have been because she saw him once outside the inn. It had been too dark to see anything then. No, there was something about his round eyes and thick rubbery lips . . .

'He's with Skunk!' Coal shouted as the truth dawned on him. 'Run!'

Of course! Mr Razzak was the fourth miner! The one who had brought Skunk up Mount Armora and told him where to camp. This was why the children had been locked in his stable. Who else would have enough local knowledge to know where to hide the Moles?

With a bellow, Mr Razzak pushed past his wife and burst out of the doorway. As he started after Coal, Harris stuck out his leg and sent him flying. Mr Razzak landed on the pavement with a loud thump. 'Nina, get that boy!' he screamed. 'We're done for if he goes to the police!'

'Stop!' Coal warned as Gogo strained against the leash, barking loudly. 'Or we'll set the dog on you!' Mrs Razzak's hands shot up and she backed away quickly.

It was now or never. The three of them and Gogo sprinted down the street, leaving the Razzaks behind with their curses.

29

The Truth about Witchcraft

Following Harris' lead, they half ran, half walked to the plaza where a large crowd had gathered. All around them, a sea of men and women stood waiting for the trial to begin, their faces drunk with anticipation.

Elven and Harris weaved through the crowd, forcing their way towards the middle of the plaza, with Coal and Gogo following behind. At the clearing next to the fountain, someone had erected a huge stack of logs. In the middle, hands tied to a large wooden stake, hair loose around her shoulder, was poor Madam Green being interrogated by Ojas. Off to the side, the captured children were kneeling on the ground, surrounded by young men with guns. Before Elven could take a step forward, she felt a tap from Coal. He shook his head at her and mouthed the word 'no'.

'Speak up, witch!' Ojas growled a few inches from Madam Green's face. 'Where have you hidden the missing girl?'

The crowd fell silent, straining to hear the answer.

'I am innocent.' Madam Green's voice rang through the plaza, loud and firm. If she was afraid, she did not show it. Even in this unceremonious position, she held her chin up, proud and defiant.

'If you insist on lying,' Ojas said, 'we'll have to call a witness.'

'That's me! That's me!' shouted a voice that Elven had come to dislike. She turned and saw the store manager pushing his way to the front of the crowd, accompanied by the burly man in dungarees. 'I saw her supernatural powers with my own eyes. These children were calling out for help when I stumbled upon the witch's coven. She locks them in cages with her wolves!'

To Elven's dismay, the store manager began retelling his story to the raptured crowd.

'And what do you say to that, witch?' Ojas asked, triumphant.

'Stuff and nonsense!' Madam Green said. 'The voices he heard were from the very parrots you Armorians had abandoned. The howls were those of the dogs you cast off. I rescue your pets when you get tired of them, and now you turn on me like wolves on a sheep.'

A ripple of surprise passed through the crowd. Several townsfolk reacted with indignation; others pulled the brims of their hats over their burning faces.

'But the night I lost my way, I shot an arrow at her and it bounced right off!' the store manager insisted.

Madam Green turned to him with a frown. 'An arrow?'

'You didn't die!' The store manager pointed his finger accusingly at Madam Green. 'I'm a good marksman. My arrow could have killed you—'

A look of recognition came over Madam Green's face. 'So, you were the one who took aim at me! I remember that arrow all right.' She narrowed her eyes in disgust. 'There are two doors to my house—one wooden and the other glass. I was standing behind the glass door when you fired your arrow.'

'You lie!' the store manager yelled.

'If there's anyone who doesn't believe me,' Madam Green said, 'he can come see for himself.'

'It's a trap,' Ojas cautioned. 'Fall under her spell and you'll be her slave forever.' He gestured dramatically at Ryan and the others. 'Stories we grew up with don't sprout from thin air. Look at the children we found on the mountain. Look how thin and starved they are. Why were they there, against their will? For too long, we've let this monster get away with her unnatural acts. If we don't stop her today, this town will forever live in terror!'

'No to black magic!' someone shouted.

Cries of outrage punctuated the air. Young children huddled against their parents, sobbing in fear. The crowd's hysteria reached a fever pitch.

Ojas held up a torch and advanced towards the pyre. In the dwindling light, his expression was one of pure evil. If he had only one goal, it was to destroy Madam Green.

'Burn the witch!' the crowd chanted. 'Burn the witch!'

Elven could bear it no more. Breaking away from the anonymity of the masses, she ran forward and planted herself between Madam Green and Ojas.

'Stop!' she cried, holding up her hands. 'I live with Madam Green and she's not a monster.'

'You!' Ojas exclaimed. 'You're the missing—' He was about to say more when the store manager stepped up and whispered in his ear. Ojas frowned as he listened, but a crafty smile soon spread across his face. 'Well, well, well, the Lord has delivered our living proof.' He marched over to Elven and clamped his hand over her wrist. '*This* is the half-Mawoli girl we freed from the witch's lair! This is the half-breed whose *blood* the witch imbibes to strengthen her power!' Elven flinched as Ojas thrust the torch in her face. 'Look at her! Look at her mongrel features.'

Elven's cheeks blistered from the heat of a thousand suns. *How did Ojas guess I'm half Native? What did the store manager say to him?* Her most shameful secret, which she had so carefully protected, was suddenly out in the open. She recoiled from the crowd, scared of the hatred she would see in their faces. If she had a spade, she would dig a hole right there and then. She would rather bury herself alive than face their scrutiny.

'No,' she begged. 'Please, no.'

'No what?' Ojas sneered, his torch flitting dangerously close to her face. 'No—you do not live with the witch and, therefore, have no business disrupting our trial? Or no—you're not a half-breed, a chimera, a mutt, but simply one of those she keeps in cages?'

'I . . . I . . .'

'Elven . . .' She heard Madam Green calling out to her. 'Leave. Save yourself.'

But I can't let them burn you alive.

'Let them go!' a man said in a deep baritone. Elven turned and saw Mr Bora step out from the edge of the crowd. His hair was wild but his expression steady. He met Elven's eyes and gave her a small nod. Yes! Kraw had delivered the message!

Ojas gave a hoot. 'If it isn't the world-famous Mawoli chef himself!' Letting go of Elven, he pretended to prostrate himself before Mr Bora. 'Saving your own kind, eh?'

'It's none of your business what the girl is or isn't,' Mr Bora said.

'It's his business, of course it is,' the store manager countered. 'It's Armora's business to know what goes on in the mountain.'

'The half-Mawoli girl is proof of the bloodsucker's guilt,' Ojas said, waving his torch at Madam Green. 'Why else would a woman be living with a bunch of children who are not related to her?'

'Because she is kind, and she is compassionate,' Mr Bora answered. 'But I don't expect you to understand that.'

Tears trickled down Elven's face. If nobody could see Madam Green's goodness then how would this all end? Where was the light at the end of the tunnel? It was then that Mr Bora's words came back to her: *If we unshackle ourselves from the past, we'll all have a brighter future.*

In summer, she had dismissed his advice as they sped towards Bowler Hat Lake, her mind occupied entirely by the Puzzle Box. Now, for the first time, she suddenly saw how her perceived 'humiliation' was the direct result of her childhood. From an early age, she had been taught by Director Hammond to reject the Natives and all they stood for. She was told to bring down Mawoli traditions in order to elevate Western ideals, to despise her skin tone and be ashamed of who she was or who she might be.

But why? Why should she cower? Why should she aspire to be a colonizer when she was a true daughter of this land? Her skin should be a tribute to the sun's glory, not a source of shame. She suddenly understood that being free had nothing to do with running away or opening a Puzzle Box.

Being free was embracing herself for who she was. Who she could be.

'Yes, it's true I'm half Mawoli!' Elven straightened her back, her voice sailing above the chatter. 'My mother, a Westerner, eloped with a Native to give birth to me. After she died, I was sent to an orphanage not far from here. That was all the life I knew until I ran away and was taken in by Madam Green. For more than three months now, I've lived on Mount Armora. According to these men, my benefactor is actually a witch who cuts me up every night to suck on my blood.' She paused, sweeping her eyes over the townsfolk. 'If this is true,' she shouted, 'why isn't there a single scar on me?'

Before anyone could stop her, Elven had stripped off her long dress so that all she was clad in was a white cotton slip. The crowd let out a collective gasp.

'If she's a witch, where are my scars?' Elven demanded, raising her arms at Ojas. 'Where are my scars?'

For once, Ojas was speechless.

'Fellas!' a voice cut through the silence. 'Surely you're not planning a barbecue in the middle of our beautiful plaza?'

At this, the crowd parted. A bear of a man with a handlebar moustache and tanned leathery skin swaggered into sight. On his shirt was a bright metal star; on his right hip, a pistol sat in a worn leather holster. The police chief signalled to one of his men who clambered on the logs to untie Madam Green.

'You're letting her go?' Ojas shook his head incredulously. 'After all our efforts?'

'I'm merely restoring her to a position of dignity,' the chief replied. A sudden wave of excitement spread through the crowd. But it was not the chief who had caught the townsfolk's attention but the slim, handsome man in the white suit walking next to him.

'It's the governor!' a young lady swooned.

Elven suspected that this was not a coincidence. Mr Bora knew the governor and must have asked him for help. The question was: would this powerful man believe the words of one against many?

The governor raised his hand and stepped forward to address the town.

'Those of you old enough to recall the Noury Emporium,' he said in an elegant accent, 'must surely remember Mrs Noury, as she was known then. For many years, she has shown this town nothing but civility and kindness. I myself have known her since we were children attending the same school in Kenden. Her parents and grandparents were hard-working, middle-class folks, not wizards and witches like you imagine.

'If there is any sorcery she is capable of,' the governor added, 'it is only that of conjuring away your unwanted pets. This is an ordinary woman, Armorians. I ask you to look to facts, not hearsay. You are better than this.'

He walked over to the pyre and held up his hand to help Madam Green down. One by one, the young men lowered their guns, their expressions uncertain. Elven pulled on her dress and ran forward to give Madam Green a bone-crunching hug.

'Not so fast!' Ojas shouted, waving his rifle at her. 'What about those children we found in the cages? You can't explain that away!'

'It's not a cage! It's an aviary!' Elven cried in exasperation. 'The children were kidnapped and forced to dig for gold on Mount Armora. Madam Green and I rescued them.'

Disbelief rippled through the plaza.

'Kidnapped?' The chief raised his eyebrows in surprise. 'By who?'

The gaze of the crowd shifted to the children, then back to Madam Green.

'Gold miners,' Madam Green said. 'Four men from out of town—'

'Three,' Elven interrupted. 'Mr Razzak was one of them and there's another Armorian who's been helping them.'

'Look at her smearing Razzak's good name,' Ojas sneered. 'What proof do they have?'

Proof? Elven glared at him. *Haven't I shown you enough proof?*

'The man who kidnapped my friends is called Morodon-Gore,' she said, clenching her fists. 'All you need to do is contact Goldsmith College. Search him up—'

'There's no need for that,' Coal cut in. He walked out of the crowd and pointed his finger at a figure behind the fountain. 'There he is, right there.'

30

The Villain Unmasked

Loud boos erupted from the crowd.

'What nonsense!'

'Slander!'

'Why would the mayor do that?'

The governor took a step towards Coal, whose face had turned a sickly white. 'Young man,' he said in a low voice, 'that man's name is Gordon Moore. He's the mayor of Armora.'

'I'd recognize his face anywhere.' Coal crossed his arms. Next to him, Gogo let out a low growl. 'His name is Morodon-Gore. I'll never forget how he tricked me into being a slave!'

Elven looked at Coal, bewildered. Had her friend gone mad?

'You realize this is a serious accusation you're making,' the governor warned.

'It's him,' Coal insisted. 'Those miners were working for him. He posed as the headmaster of a non-existent boarding school, tricked our orphanage director into releasing us into his care and forced us to work in gold mines. He also kidnapped the two Mawoli children from their village. Who knows how many others are still locked up?'

'Obviously this is a plot by my enemies to destroy my reputation,' the mayor said. 'The boy has been bribed by someone to defame me in public. If you wish to waste your time with liars, I won't stop you, governor.' He threw up his hands. 'But I've had enough of this circus!'

The mayor turned to walk away but the police chief was there blocking his way. 'Come on now, Gordon. What's the hurry? Let's talk it through, shall we?' He clamped his large hand on the mayor's shoulder and marched him gently, but insistently, towards the children.

'By golly, it *is* him!' shouted Ryan, jumping up. 'He had a fake beard on, but I could recognize him anywhere!'

'You horrid man!' cried Matthew. 'You almost killed us!'

'You took us from our tribal land!' Anika shouted before breaking into sobs.

'Stupid kids, the man who wronged you is called Morodon-Gore,' the mayor yelled. 'You heard your friend. This has nothing to do with me.'

Elven tried to recall the day when Harris had been given a dressing down by the mayor. Hadn't she had the feeling that he was somewhat familiar, even though she had never met him before?

Best not to offend them. We don't want trouble from Gordon.
Gordon Moore.

Morodon-Gore.

As Elven repeated the names in her head, it suddenly became crystal clear what the mayor had done. It was just like him to use a trick he had picked up from Master Takuno for a twisted purpose.

'The pseudonym Morodon-Gore is just an anagram of Gordon Moore!' Elven burst out. 'A clever trick to hide his real identity. Ask Mr Razzak! He knows the truth.'

A deep frown cut across the chief's forehead. 'Mayor Moore,' he said. 'You now have six witnesses accusing you of kidnap and attempted murder. And if Mr Razzak collaborates with what they say . . .'

'Why?' the governor asked, shaking his head. 'Why did you do it, Gordon? You don't need the money.'

'Money?' A sneer contorted Mayor Moore's face. 'What do you know about money? You grew up with a silver spoon in your mouth.' He started laughing hysterically. 'Do you remember the gold rush? My father came here believing he could be part of that dream. But just as he was getting started, the protests shut it all down. He lost his entire life savings—every single cent he had invested—and with that, his sanity. Do you have any idea what it was like to see the person you loved destroyed in the name of a greater good?' The mayor spat on the ground. 'The gold on Mount Armora belongs to me! I have a right to recover what my father was owed—'

'Razzak's here!' someone shouted.

At that, the innkeeper rushed up to the mayor, panting. 'Give me my daughter,' he demanded. 'You took her, too, didn't you?'

'I have nothing to do with your daughter's disappearance,' Mayor Moore hissed in a low voice. 'Do get a grip on yourself. If I go down, you go down too.'

'I don't care any more,' Mr Razzak cried, his eyes wild. 'I just want my child back!'

'You fool!' Mayor Moore snapped. 'If your child is as stupid as you then this town is better off without another imbecile.'

The innkeeper's fist landed on the mayor's face with a sickening crack. The crowd went berserk as Mayor Moore fell against the governor, knocking him off his feet. Pushing against the governor, Mayor Moore sprang up and charged at Mr Razzak, wrestling him to the ground. With a shriek, Mrs Razzak, who had been watching from the side, grabbed a log from the pyre and came running. Just as she was about to swing it at the mayor's head, a policeman stepped in and grabbed her by the shoulder. In the struggle that ensued, the log flew into the crowd, causing someone to yell out in pain.

The governor exchanged a sharp look with the chief, who fired a shot in the air. The crowd fell back, and the chief's men stepped in and tore the two men away from each other.

Sprawled on the ground, Mrs Razzak had disintegrated into tears and shrieks. The governor tried to help her up but she would have none of it.

'There is no justice!' Mrs Razzak screamed, tearing at her hair. 'My daughter is missing and no one cares!'

'I have searched every house in this town,' said the chief to the inconsolable woman. 'Every single one I can enter. For the love of God, I—'

'Then, there are some you've not searched?' Elven interrupted.

'I do not think our respectable townsfolk have anything to gain from kidnapping the innkeeper's daughter,' he said, ignoring her question. 'If she can't be found then maybe she wasn't kidnapped. Maybe she ran away.'

'How long has your daughter been missing?' Harris asked Mr Razzak who now sported a reddish bruise on his jaw.

'Since Wednesday afternoon.' He took out a handkerchief from his pocket and wiped the blood from his lips.

'We had a quarrel,' Mrs Razzak said, between sobs.

'What did you argue about?' Elven asked. 'If you don't mind me asking.'

'Food . . .' Mrs Razzak buried her face in her palms. 'It's silly now that I think back about it. She was obsessed with that Mawoli snack . . . sticky potato or something.'

'Sticky yam balls?' asked Elven.

'Yes, that's the one. She was always going to the plaza to wait for the pushcart vendor. Wanted to try all of them, you see. When the vendor stopped coming to the plaza, she insisted on going around town to look for the cart.'

'We wouldn't let her,' Mr Razzak added, 'so she stormed out.'

'And that was the last we saw of her,' Mrs Razzak said, tearing up again.

'But you don't think she ran away?' Elven asked.

'Absolutely not!' Mr Razzak glared at them, offended. 'She may be rash but she's not stupid!'

A curious idea struck Elven.

'Have you seen Mama Monga recently?' she asked Harris.

'Not for a long time,' he replied. 'The last time I had a craving, I had to go all the way to Alluvium to find her.'

'Coal, make sure Madam Green and the other kids are all right,' Elven said. Then, beckoning to the Razzaks, she said, 'We need to check out Master Takuno's workshop.'

31

The Temptation of Sticky Yam Balls

Elven and Harris took off for the neighbourhood of Alluvium, followed by the Razzaks. As they were waiting for the adults to catch up, Elven spotted Mama Monga in the distance carrying a suitcase. With a yell, they sprinted up to her.

'God Almighty!' Mama Monga exclaimed, dropping her luggage. 'Can't a woman take a holiday without being harassed by hungry customers?'

'A holiday?' Elven asked. 'But what about your pushcart?'

'I've sold it!' Mama Monga let out a peal of laughter. 'Along with all my yam balls.'

'So you didn't sell any sticky yam balls to a little girl between Wednesday and today?' Elven asked. 'She's about my age and has dark hair—'

'Nah, in fact it was on Wednesday that I met this fellow outside Takuno's place. He said he needed to haul away rubbish from the workshop and asked me if he could borrow my cart.'

Elven exchanged a glance with Harris. 'And you let him?'

'Of course not, I had a business to run!' Mama Monga said. 'But the fellow whipped out a ton of cash and offered to buy up both the cart and my sticky yam balls. So I sold off everything, and now, I'm retired! As free as a bird.'

'But you can't just retire!' Harris scrunched up his face in distress. 'How will I get my sticky yam ball fix?'

'I'm afraid that's a tragedy you'll have to live with, young man,' Mama Monga said in a deadpan voice. 'Or you could try your luck at Takuno's workshop. I passed the fellow on the way out. Catch him before he leaves and maybe he'll resell you some.'

Elven and Harris bade goodbye to Mama Monga and headed past the old huts and overgrown fields. As Master Takuno's workshop came into view, they saw a man hitching a donkey to what looked like Mama Monga's pushcart. But instead of sticky yam balls, the cart was stacked high with bags and crates.

The man spun around at the sound of their footsteps, his ponytail swishing through the air.

Moldylocks?

Elven braked to a stop, causing Harris to collide into her.

'Yes, children?' The surprised expression on Moldylock's face quickly transformed to irritation. 'What do you want?'

Instinctively, Elven hid her left hand behind her back. Moldylocks did not seem to recognize her and she did not want to put him on his guard.

'Well?' Moldylocks asked, impatient.

Elven opened her mouth to speak but the words seemed to be stuck to her throat. Something wasn't right. Why was Moldylocks still hanging around Armora? And right outside Takuno's workshop too! Was he still working for Gordon Moore?

'Mama Monga told us you might sell us some sticky yam balls,' Harris said.

'Mama who?' Moldylocks asked with a frown. Just as quickly, his expression changed into one of pure cunning. 'Ah, the yam balls! Children love them, don't they? Sure, I have lots left.'

'Hooray!' Harris exclaimed, pumping his fist in the air.

A smile spread across Moldylocks' face. 'Why don't you come in and choose one you like?'

Harris was about to take a step forward when Elven grabbed his arm. 'It's him, you idiot! He's the one!' she hissed.

'Of course he is,' Harris said, shaking her off. 'Now, don't stand between me and my sticky yam balls.'

Elven watched, horrified, as Harris skipped up to the door and pushed it open. In one swift motion, Moldylocks pushed Harris into the workshop, slamming the door shut.

Then, turning to Elven, he said, 'If it isn't the freak with eleven fingers.'

'Who are you calling a freak?' Elven glared back. She could hear Harris yelling for help. 'Let my friend out and hand over the missing girl,' she said.

Moldylocks snorted and took a step towards her. 'Very brave of you to make demands when you're about to join them for a spot of mining in the deep South . . .' Suddenly, he stopped mid-sentence, panic colouring his face. 'What the . . . who are all these people?'

Elven swung around and was startled to see the townsfolk running down Cradle Street behind the Razzaks. The two Mawoli siblings burst out of the crowd. But upon seeing Moldylocks, they froze and backed off rapidly. Soon though, Elven was surrounded by Matthew, Ginger, and Ryan.

Moldylocks stared at the children, bewildered. 'What's happening, Razzak?' he asked, turning to the innkeeper. 'Why did you bring these people here?'

'BOOM, BOOM, BOOM!' A loud banging rang out from inside the workshop.

'He's got Harris and the missing girl in there!' Elven shouted. 'He's sending them to the gold mines!'

Mr Razzak stepped up to Moldylocks and grabbed him by the collar. 'Open the door immediately!'

'What are you, crazy?' Moldylocks snarled. 'Gordon's not going to let you get away with—'

'You can tell that to him now,' growled the chief, stepping out from the crowd. Next to him was a handcuffed Mayor Moore, his hunched figure flanked by two uniformed guards. Behind them, escorted by more policemen, came Madam Green and Coal.

A guttural sound escaped from Moldylocks' mouth. He stepped back against the cart, sending a pile of books crashing to the ground.

'Mayor Moore is under arrest for the abduction and imprisonment of children,' the chief continued. 'Any person found to be aiding him in his illegal activities will be dealt with severely.'

'I . . . I did not harm the girl,' Moldylocks whined, his lips quivering like leaves in the wind. 'She's eating well and sleeping well—'

'WHAT GIRL?!!' Mayor Moore's head snapped up as he bellowed at Moldylocks. 'What in the world are you talking about?' If not for the guards, he would have jumped straight at Moldylocks.

'BOOM! BOOM! BOOM!' came the banging from the workshop.

'You told me that Skunk ran away with those orphans,' Moldylocks stuttered. 'So, I thought I'd find more workers for you. I mean, you bought this place to hold the Moles—'

'You fool!' Mayor Moore screamed. 'I said, no kids from Armora! Which part of that do you not understand?'

'So, kidnapping children outside Armora is fine?' the chief asked.

'The mayor's the real mountain witch,' Coal shouted.

Mayor Moore opened his mouth to protest, but his words were drowned out by angry shouts from the onlookers.

'Burn him!' a man yelled.

'How dare you?' Mayor Moore shouted back. 'I'm the mayor of Ar—' But then, without warning, the colour drained out of his face. His knees buckled under him and he fell to the ground, hands clutching his chest.

'Take him away quickly,' the chief commanded his staff. Then, instructing the Razzaks to stay where they were, he marched Moldylocks into the workshop.

Seconds later, a muffled cry rang out. The missing girl tore out of the workshop, weeping and stumbling into Mr and Mrs Razzak's open arms.

Elven watched the reunion, a curious mix of pride and envy swirling inside her. How many times had she imagined such a scene for herself?

'Are you all right, my dear?'

She looked up and saw Madam Green staring at her with undisguised concern. Next to her was Mr Long.

'Yes,' she replied, managing a small smile.

'Let's hope those miners never come back,' Madam Green said as they watched Moldylocks and Mr Razzak being led away by the chief.

Mr Long nodded. 'We need to educate the next generation on the environmental impact of mining.'

'Didn't you use to organize an annual Earth Day celebration?' Madam Green reminded him.

'Maybe it's time to bring that back,' Mr Long said.

'Do you know each other?' Elven asked.

Madam Green chuckled softly. 'Mr Long used to be Aimee's mathematics tutor.'

Elven's eyes widened. 'You taught Madam Green's daughter?'

'Oh yes, even at a young age, Aimee had a most analytical mind.' Mr Long's eyes softened visibly. 'If she were here today, she'd have a field day with your Puzzle Box . . .'

Their conversation was interrupted by excited squeals from the children. Harris had emerged from Takuno's workshop with a large tray of sticky yam balls, fragrant and glistening under the sun.

'Get your sticky yam balls!' he shouted. 'Sweet or salty, take your pick! Colours of the rainbow, all you can eat!'

The crowd surged forward, hands reaching eagerly for the tray. Neighbourly conversations peppered the air as the townsfolk sank their teeth into the sticky yam balls, some of them for the very first time.

'You mean you've never tried Mawoli food? You don't know what you're missing out on, old chap!'

'You know, I've always told the town council that street food can be just as delicious and healthy . . .'

'Can I have a second helping?'

The Armorians milled around, laughing and exchanging gossip. Some people from the neighbouring houses brought out beer and juice, while others contributed crackers and nuts. As night fell, the street lamps came on, lending a magical quality to the evening. An old man started strumming his guitar and another joined in with his harmonica. Before long, a street party was in full swing.

32

A Flower in Bloom

Madam Green and the children did not stay long for the festivities—they were eager to check on the house. Despite Madam Green's protest, Mr Bora insisted on escorting them home in case there were still shady characters loitering around in the dark. Lanterns swinging, the group made their way up the mountain trail, chatting about the day's exploits. The Mawoli siblings were particularly excited as they recounted their conversation with the governor, who had promised to send them back home and secure a fair trial for their parents.

'Do you think we'll be sent back to the orphanage?' Matthew asked Mr Bora.

'Not before the governor finds out what's happening behind those walls,' Mr Bora said with a grim expression.

'Director Hammond will most certainly blame us for getting the governor involved,' Ryan said in an ominous tone. 'Goodness knows what he'll do to us.'

'I'm scared,' Ginger whimpered.

'Children, the governor is good at his job,' Madam Green assured them. 'He won't send you back unless he's sure you'll be safe.'

As everyone speculated about their new lives ahead with mixed feelings, Elven reminded herself to hand Mr Bora the letter she had written to him earlier. If there was anything she could do to repay Coal, it would be to help him get an apprenticeship at Fhakawaiwai. She thought about the new revelations and the old ties that had been uncovered; about how Madam Green would forever be bound to a town that both needed and feared her. It was as if everyone had been connected by an invisible thread—the governor, Mr Long, Master Takuno, and even Gordon Moore. Elven wondered if she was part of that entanglement too. If so, who was she tied to? Had her mother left her the Puzzle Box as a way to get her here? Elven had a feeling that she was on the cusp of making an important discovery. But the harder she tried to concentrate, the more it eluded her.

At the house, Mr Bora offered to dress the children's wounds while Madam Green and Elven assessed the damage caused by the mob. Oddly, under the soft moonlight, the destruction to the property looked less severe than in the day.

'Thank heavens Gogo helped us escape from Mr Razzak,' Elven said, recounting their adventure at the inn.

Madam Green patted Gogo on the head. 'Gogo's always got this fighting spirit about him. You could see it in him even when he was just a month old.'

'You had him as a puppy? Wasn't he adopted like the others?'

Madam Green shook her head. 'I never told you this but Gogo's parents were imported into Kalimasia by the Noury Emporium as puppies. When their owner grew tired of them, they were sent to Talford's awful "shelter".'

'And it was during that trip there that you found them?'

'They were all skin and bones.' Madam Green grimaced as she recalled the memory. 'My daughter insisted on bringing them home and so we did. Talford detested them, and it was no surprise that he left them behind when he disappeared with her. But if there's a way to remember things in a positive light then I'll say that they were Aimee's final present to me.'

A gentle light shone in Madam Green's eyes as she ran her fingers down Gogo's back. 'And so even though these farewell gifts bring us both joy and sorrow, I would like to think that it is more of the former. Not unlike the Puzzle Box your mother left you, don't you feel?'

At the reminder, Elven took out the Puzzle Box from her right pocket. Then, she fished out from her left pocket the list of names she had meant to show Mr Long: Marie Enyou, Arnie Meyou, May Ourinée, Amy Ourinée, and Maiee Noury.

Noury... like Noury Emporium. Like Talford Noury.

The cursive script of her grandfather's initials flashed before her eyes: T.N.

Could T.N. stand for Talford Noury?

Elven's heart skipped a beat.

Aimee and Noury were both five-letter words.

What if she rearranged the word Maiee by moving the letter M to the middle of the name?

With trembling hands, Elven shifted the tiles this way and that until there was only one inevitable move left.

Could this be it? Could this Aimee be the same Aimee lost to Madam Green? The same Aimee who loved puzzles and whom Mr Long remembered with such fondness? The same Aimee whose nightgown she wore on her first night here?

As the letter M locked into place, Elven felt a faint shift of tension radiating through her fingers.

AIMEE NOURY

The box gave a soft click and sprang open like a flower in bloom. Elven cried out as the pieces parted to reveal a wooden locket covered with black swirls.

With trembling hands, she pried open the oval halves of the locket and held them up to the light of the lantern. Inside were two black and white photographs. On the left, a delicate-looking young woman stared out with a smile that Elven often saw in the mirror.

She looks like me, but with bigger eyes.

On the right half of the locket was another woman who was much older. A beautiful woman so regal she could be a queen. Her light-coloured hair was piled high on her head. A beauty mole marked her right cheekbone like Venus in the night sky.

Elven inhaled sharply. She held out the locket to Madam Green, her hands shaking. 'It's you! Tell me it's you!'

When Madam Green saw the photographs, she let out a gasp. 'Where did you . . .? That's me, and that's Aimee, my daughter—'

'I'm Aimee's child!' Elven cried as she pressed the lid of the Puzzle Box into Madam Green's hands.

Seeing her daughter's name, Madam Green began to weep, her shoulders slumped over from the weight of the lost decades. 'She'd kept it safe from Talford . . . after all these years.'

Elven put her arms around her grandmother. 'It's all right,' she said softly. 'I'm home now.'

She finally understood why her mother had to use an anagram. It was a trick—a clever decoy to prevent Elven's grandfather, Talford Noury, from retrieving the locket. The most dangerous place had been the safest hiding place.

'She must have returned to Armora to look for me,' Madam Green said at last. 'And when she couldn't find me, she must have had the Puzzle Box made.' She sighed and wiped her eyes. 'I never should have gone up the mountain.'

'But you had no choice. One can only pedal forward, not backward.'

Madam Green's moist eyes twinkled like stars. 'You're learning, my grandchild.' She turned over the locket and murmured, 'Why, I never!'

'What is it?'

A curious look came over Madam Green's tear-stained face. 'Come,' she said as she hurried towards the house. 'Ariki! Anika!' she called out the moment they stepped in. When the siblings came running, Madam Green held out the closed locket to them. 'Does the design mean anything to you?'

The siblings let out a loud exclamation as they crowded around.

'What?' Elven said, her heart in her throat.

'Where did this come from?' Ariki asked, his voice suddenly solemn.

'From my mother.' Elven took the locket from Madam Green, half afraid of what she would hear. Her grandfather had called her father a 'good-for-nothing Native'. Did the design represent a Mawoli gang? Was her father a criminal?

'These triple twists here,' Anika said pointing to the motifs, 'represent the joining together of two people, from two different cultures.'

'For eternity,' Ariki said. 'He must have given this locket to your mother as a symbol of love.'

'So it's good?' Elven asked in a whisper.

'Of course!' the siblings exclaimed in unison.

'May I take a closer look?' Ariki asked. When Elven nodded yes, he took the locket in his hand and flipped it around. He let out a whistle, his pinkie finger tracing the sharp triangular patterns radiating out from the centre of the locket. 'These spikes represent courage.'

'The mark of the bravest in a tribe,' Anika added. 'Someone who made a difference to his people.'

'Elven, your father must have been a hero,' Madam Green said, her eyes shining like emeralds.

Ariki held out the locket with both palms as if it were sacred. Elven closed her hands over Ariki's tightly. She felt as if her chest would burst. All this time she had pictured her father as weak and cowardly because of her grandfather's letter. But with the locket proving otherwise, she could now hold her head up high.

'Come to the Southland with us,' Anika urged. 'You won't have to face any discrimination like you do here. With your father's reputation, our villagers will treat you as their own. Acceptance is what you've been searching for all along, isn't it? The reason why you left the orphanage.'

Acceptance?

Yes, she had always wanted that. But entering a Mawoli village would mean giving up the part of her that wasn't Mawoli, the part of her that came from her mother, from Madam Green, and—as her eyes fell on the painting—the generations before them.

It struck her that she was not unlike a Puzzle Box, a unique work of art created by different types of wood interlocked together. Just as her Puzzle Box was not maple, teak, or cherry, she was not Westerner, Mawoli, or Cantorean. She was none of them, yet all of them.

She was Elven, and she was loved.

That elusive thing, that indescribable feeling.

Love was her mother keeping the locket safe for her. It was Coal risking his future for her. Love was Master Takuno betting on the heart's permanence. It was Madam Green taking her in at her darkest hour.

Love was the loyal Gogo who stood by her, the bountiful garden, the talkative parrots, the majestic mountain—she had cared for them and they had loved her back, unconditionally and unapologetically.

'No, not acceptance,' Elven said. 'Love.' She smiled and took her grandmother's hand. 'I've finally found love.'

Epilogue

Elven raised the round, woven lid of the bamboo steamer and poured the purple batter into the square metal container sitting in it. This was the last layer of her rainbow kueh, a modification of a traditional Mawoli recipe that used rice flour and coconut milk. She had toiled tirelessly for weeks to perfect the seven dye colours using only natural ingredients sourced locally. Some of them grew in the wild, like the butterfly pea flowers that gave her batter a purplish hue, while others like red cabbage, saffron, and spinach were harvested from Mr Bora's garden.

Today was a big day—the launch party for her cookbook: *The Best of Mawoli Desserts*. In it, Elven included not only the recipes that Mr Bora's restaurant was famous for, but obscure ones that she and Madam Green had collected from the tribes in the Southland. Surveying the delectable spread in Fhakawaiwai's kitchen, Elven gave a tired but satisfied smile. She had been up since four o'clock, and the adrenaline coursing through her veins was just starting to wear off. Still, it was worth it. She could not wait to surprise the guests with the rice pudding, sticky yam balls, and more.

Strolling over to the large cardboard box in the corner, she lifted the lid and removed the tissue paper at the top. Inside were fifty copies of the cookbook pre-ordered by Fhakawaiwai's regular customers. Elven picked one up, still not quite believing that her name was on the cover. Inhaling the smell of fresh ink, she sat down at the table and leafed through the pages, admiring the illustrations—each one a reminder of her days in the capital.

How things had changed in the last three years! Shortly after Gordon Moore's arrest, the governor made good on his word and reunited Ariki and Anika with their parents. He also commissioned an independent investigation into the conditions of the orphanage and fired Director Hammond, Mrs Monteiro, and other caretakers who had been abusive and negligent. A new director was appointed swiftly and the teaching materials revamped to include the history of the Mawoli people. At the same time, following the widespread publicity of the criminal trial involving Moore and the miners, several citizens had stepped forward to volunteer as foster parents for Ryan, Matthew, and Ginger. At Mr Bora's urging, Madam Green, Elven, and Coal finally moved to Kenden to work at the restaurant—Coal as his apprentice, Madam Green at the front of house, and Elven assisting the pastry chef. It was in this very kitchen that she began toying with the idea of a Mawoli cookbook.

'Time to get ready for the party,' Madam Green said, appearing at the doorway. She was dressed in a traditional Cantorean costume—a flowing robe of olive silk and a tricoloured headscarf woven with green, blue, and yellow threads. In her hands, she held a small bottle and paintbrush.

Elven rolled up her sleeves and held out her right arm to Madam Green who came to sit beside her. As the sun rose in the eastern window, Madam Green dipped the brush into the bottle and brought it towards her granddaughter. Stroke by stroke, petal by petal, bright blue maliaki flowers began to bloom on Elven's golden skin.

Acknowledgements

I completed the first draft of this book in 2016 and, for close to a decade, never thought I would see it bound and printed. So, if you are an aspiring writer, don't give up! If you want something badly enough (like me) and you are willing to put in the work, it will happen to you.

Publishing is a long journey, and I would not have been able to stay on this path without the encouragement from my fellow writers and the readers who purchased my books.

To the team at Penguin Random House SEA, Nora Nazerene Abu Bakar and Amberdawn Manaois: Thank you for believing in me and helping me make this manuscript the best that it can be. I am grateful for the opportunity to work with you.

To Jay Lehmann, one of the most talented and determined writers I know: Thank you for reading anything I throw at you and cheering me on. You are the best writing buddy anyone can ask for.

I am thankful to these individuals who have read earlier versions of this novel: Suzanne Morrone, Jessica Bayliss, Emily Mangini, John Rudolph, and Jessica Vitalis. This book would not have been possible without your input.

Lastly, special thanks to my husband who is a synopsis wizard and a brilliant wordsmith.